UNLIKELY ALPHAS

A FATED MATES OMEGAVERSE REVERSE HAREM
EPIC FANTASY ROMANCE

HUNTED FAE 2

MONA BLACK

UNLIKELY ALPHAS

Awakening as a Fae-blooded omega means I'm hunted by the Empire. My wondrous womb is dangerous, apparently. Perhaps they think I will bring back the lost Fae race by myself?

Well, not entirely by myself, of course. Even on the run, I'm already collecting alphas for my clan, and they are gorgeous.

You can't have them, they're mine.

If only they would accept their role as my fated mates and mate me already!

As it turns out, I have a knack for collecting the most unlikely alphas. So far I have a priest and an army commander – and now I've been abducted by a berserker, a Wildman.

Surely he can't be one of my fated mates, right?

...and yet.

I don't even know if he's a man or a beast, and whether we'll rejoin my other two reluctant mates or not.

Or if we'll make it to the south and be safe from the Empire's wrath, free to build a new life.

Hopefully all together.

Unless I find more of my fated mates before that, and the

way things are going, I might have an entire troupe by the time we cross the border.

If we make it there alive.

And if my heat doesn't start, first.

What could go wrong, right?

*UNLIKELY ALPHAS is a full-length epic fantasy reverse harem omegaverse romance, meaning the main character has more than one love interest. This is book two of four, and it ends on a cliffhanger. There is a happily ever after at the end of the series. All four books have already been written.

In this series, the heroine will assemble her harem throughout the first three books. It contains some love-hate adult themes, foul language and explicit content with darker elements, as well as MM relationships. For 18+ only.

This book uses alternating points of view.*

Trigger warnings: abandonment by parent, slavery, reference to violence and genocide, betrayal of friend, race discrimination, prejudice, some physical abuse, mention of death (outside the harem).

What to expect in this series:

 Omega awakening

 FMC collects her men throughout the series

 Fated mates

 Scenting, marking, knotting, heats and ruts

 MM relationships

 Blind alpha in harem

 Grumpy/sunshine

 Men fall for her (almost) immediately

 Multi POV

 Epic fantasy setting

1

ARIADNE

"Put me down! You big oaf, I said, put me down right this instant! I'm not a log for you to carry like that, you..." I gasp when the Wildman who abducted me from the bank of the stream where I had been resting with my maybe-but-not-quite-fated mates, Finnen and Taj, starts running—with me slung over his shoulder, my legs and arms bouncing. "Put me down!"

He's freakishly strong, I think dizzily, to be carrying me while running through meadows and groves, his shoulder broad and padded with muscle under my middle.

My aching middle, which had been aching even before he threw me over his shoulder and took off. It's the stirrings of my heat, it seems, this aching and clenching deep inside my belly. The precursors of my ending.

Because I'm an omega whose mates don't ever get around to sleeping with her!

Gods help me.

And not just any omega, according to the Council of the Twelve and the Temple Synod: no, I may be a Fae-blood omega, and even worse, one of the prophesied omegas who might change the route of history by bringing back the presumed-dead race of the Fae. A race supposed to be extinct since the war all those centuries ago, but whose blood still runs in the veins of many of us in the Anchar Empire, in some more than others.

"Stop!" I bang on his back with my hands. "Put me down!"

But he keeps running.

Taj said I'm his mate, and so is Finnen, and judging from their delicious scents and the way my body responds to them I'm tempted to say he's right.

Then again, my body seems to respond the same way to this specific Wildman's scent. The same intense, belly-aching, netherparts-wetting, screaming-need exact way.

When he's not kidnapping me and running about with my anatomy hanging off him like a rolled-up rug, at least. And no matter how much my body wants him, how it makes me want to climb the man like a tree, it doesn't change the fact that he's a fearsome berserker whose name I don't even know, who attacked us already once and who's now carrying me away from the two men I've fallen for, heading to the Gods know where.

Yeah, my heart belongs to them, like it or not, to the arrogant, dogmatic priest and the rogue army Commander, but my body...

My body obviously wants more.

It wants this growling beast of a man who's skidding down a slope and then climbing another.

Hills. We have reached hills. There was a hill nearby where we escaped from the army men.

The Commander's men, and yeah, this is confusing for me, too, but apparently Commander Taj has made his choice. Or so he said when he joined us today and now I'm already...

I draw a shuddering breath, suddenly close to tears.

Goddess save me.

I'm already far from them. I've already lost them, before I even had them.

This is ridiculous. My body's reactions and my emotions are ridiculous. Which may be typical of an omega about to enter her first heat but I doubt an omega is supposed to do that while running for her life and passing from one dangerous situation to another.

With her potential mates not sure they are her mates or that they want to consummate their relationship. Or not try to kill each other.

Why couldn't I have one day, one frigging day to talk to them, figure this out?

Gods, this unholy ride is killing me. I can't breathe. My ribs hurt. My heart is breaking. "Put me down, put me down," I whisper, a sob caught in my throat. "Ow..."

Surprisingly, he slows down.

At last.

Turning my head from side to side, I try to see where we are. It's another shelter, I realize as he walks inside, his steps echoing against stone walls. A cave, carved out of the rock. Water trickles nearby, maybe on the outer wall, and I expect it to be freezing, but it's not. Furs and leathers cover up one corner of the cave.

That's where he kneels down and hauls me off him to lay me on the furs, more gently than I'd ever have thought possible.

Still, what breath I have left is knocked out of me when my back hits the pallet and I'm left staring up at him.

So close. He's closer than ever before, and the blue eyes gazing down at me are magnetizing, a magnetic sky blue, peering between the long ropes of his locks. Crouched over me, his hands planted on the furs on either side of my body, he looks like he's about to attack.

But he remains still as a statue, only his gaze flickering,

moving from my face to my chest and back up—and his scent rolls over me, along with his gaze, making my insides curl with desire.

Oh, Gods...

"Who are you?" I whisper. "Why did you take me? What do you want with me?"

The Drakoryas—another name for the berserkers, apparently—sniffs at me, pale brows drawing together. He growls softly, baring his teeth, and though they're not blackened like the other berserker's who came at me earlier, they still look awfully sharp. Bowing his head, he sniffs at my neck and I jerk away.

I make a small sound, pressing my back to the furs as if I can sink into them and disappear. He scares me as much as he arouses me. There's something about him, about the breadth of his shoulders and chest, the hard line of his jaw, the sharp blue gaze and that air of wildness about him that excites me almost as much as his spicy scent.

With another soft growl, he sits back on his heels, then jumps to his feet and stalks toward the exit of the cave.

He's going to leave me alone here? For some reason, the thought frightens me more.

"Wait!" I sit up, curling an arm around my aching middle. "Is this your home? Is this where you live?"

He stops at the entrance, bracing one hand on the rock wall, tilting his head to the side as if listening, the way Finnen often does. He really is tall, definitely at least as tall as Taj and Finnen. He's not wearing breeches under the leather and fur girdle he has on—I wonder if he has any sort of undergarment below or... nothing?—and above his short leather boots, his legs are thick with muscle and sinew.

"Do you even speak?" I ask. "Do you understand what I'm saying? Or do you just growl at people and smash things?"

He takes a step outside the cave—and I get up hastily, stagger toward him.

"Don't go, don't leave me here! I can't stand not knowing what is going on, what you want from me. Please..." And his scent rolls over me again as he turns back around, my core tightening, tightening until I drop back to my knees, barely feeling the bone-jarring impact. "Ow. It hurts."

He's beside me in a flash. He grabs me, pushes me down on the pallet, on the furs that smell like him, and the texture sends shivers through me. His big hands hold me down as I try to curl around the pain, and he growls, showing off those sharp teeth again.

"What are you doing?" I breathe.

He's wedged between my legs again, pressing me down with the weight of his body, and when he starts tearing at my clothes, I slap at his hands. He doesn't seem to take notice and fear collides with panic, making me bite and struggle.

"Get off me! You brute! Get off!"

But as his scent winds around me tighter, I grab his shoulders and try to pull him down to me. Goddess, my body is fighting my mind, and I want him, need him to kiss me, bite me, take me, spread me—

"Where?" he asks, and it takes me a long moment to realize he has actually spoken, his voice rusty as if he hasn't been using it much, the word not much more than a growl.

I still, staring up at him, at his blue eyes with their light silver flecks. "What? Where what?"

"Hurt. Where?"

I'm staring at him, open-mouthed. "You do speak the common tongue. Why didn't you say so? Why—?"

"Hurt. Where!"

"Okay, okay. Sheesh." I'm too stunned to care about the pain right now but I plant a hand on his chest—hard and muscular under the furs—then shove a little. "It's my belly."

"Belly."

"Yes." When he lifts himself a little, giving me some room, I place my hand on my belly. "Here, see?"

"Belly," he growls, glaring down at my body as if it offended him. "Pain."

"Yeah." Well, he can speak, though it seems it's only a few words. "Pain. What is your name? You do have a name, right?"

"You in pain," he says mulishly, and look at that, he's strung three words together.

"Yes, I am. My name is Ariadne. What's yours? What's—?"

He grabs the shirt Taj gave me with one hand and tears it open. I gape at him as the laces snap and fabric rips, seams giving way, and then he throws away a handful of scraps to leave me naked from the waist up.

My nipples pebble instantly and his gaze is drawn to them. He slides one rough hand over my ribcage and taps one nipple with his forefinger, like a Temple cat playing with shadows.

I gasp, feeling it all the way into my core. I arch a little on the pallet—which only serves to press my throbbing, wet nether regions against his crotch.

And a very thick, long, hard cock.

Oh, sweet goddess...

"Where hurts?" he asks again, but he sounds distracted now, shifting against me, his finger rubbing over my nipple.

His erection is hot, or maybe I'm the one who's on fire. I lift my hips as much as I can to rub against it, and he groans, a deep, rumbling sound of need that shoots through me, making me reach for him. I'm drowning in need.

Grabbing the hanging tails of fur hanging off him, I yank him down. With a startled huff, he lies on top of me, catching himself on his elbows before he crushes me, and we both gasp when that presses his cock—his obviously naked cock—very firmly between my legs.

Oh crap.

So frigging good.

Stop this, I tell myself. *Push him away. He's a savage and a brute, the man who abducted you, and you're rubbing on him like a cat in heat.*

And on that point, though you may be going into heat, just like a cat, you're not your body's slave. You have your own mind, you're a practical, rational person, a Temple acolyte who's lived her life with discipline and form.

Get it?

It doesn't matter.

I can't help myself.

His long locks tickle my cheeks as I lift my head and press my mouth to his, powerless against the onslaught of arousal and lust. Firm lips, his thin beard scratching my chin, teeth clacking against mine, his taste spicier than his scent with a touch of honey underneath the zing.

Artume, oh, yes, this is so good...

... but he pulls back with a grunt, eyes round like saucers, a flush on his cheekbones.

Then he's off me and out of the cave like a shot, quicker than you can say *arrow*, his steps echoing long after he's gone.

If I *had* an arrow, though, I'd have thrown it at him.

Dammit.

What's an omega got to do around here to get laid? Seriously. I need a thick cock in this wet pussy, guys. An alpha cock. Something I never thought I'd say in a million years.

I don't think I've ever even used the word *cock* in a conversation in all my life.

Yeah, I'm getting desperate. Can you tell?

Even my savage kidnapper won't do me. Is it something about me that puts men off? I ask you. What will it take for my alphas to accept me?

2

ARIADNE

Sleep overtakes me as I lie among the furs. I had meant to get up and go after him, demand he take me back, or at least to run away. But these past days—weeks?—have worn me out. I'm exhausted, hungry, thirsty, in pain.

In despair.

I dream of the Temple at the fort, of Artume's statue and severe face, of the council room and Councilor Kaidan's leer—then of burning cities and dragons flying overhead like streaks of fire.

I wake up panting, disoriented and alone. Dark rock with golden veins arches over me, plants growing in the cracks. Water trickles outside, and the scent of wet stone and spices fills my nose.

Spices.

Drakoryas.

The events of the previous day filter back into my mind as I sit up. I glance down at my bare breasts and shiver.

Where is he?

Light is spilling into the cave from the opening. The night

has passed. Did he just leave me here and go hunting, or whatever it is berserkers do when not abducting girls or fighting in the Empire's army?

"Hey! Where are you?" I keep my voice low as I step out of the cave, my hands over my bare breasts, noticing in passing signs of human habitation: a metal pot, a wooden spoon, a kind of wooden bench by the wall. "Berserker!"

An animal wouldn't have utensils, I think. An animal wouldn't have language. Finnen and Taj were wrong.

Yet he did kidnap me.

And was concerned to know where I hurt.

"Dragon-kin, they call themselves." Finnen had said that. *"Wild men without taboos or ethics."*

Goddess, I miss him. And Taj. I hope they're okay. I wonder what they will do.

Come after us, that's what they'll do. I just know it in my heart. They wouldn't sit on their asses and let this Wildman take me.

But how will they track us down? Where am I?

I blink in the watery morning sunlight, then blink again.

Wow. It's a dreamy spot on the side of a rocky hill. The water trickling down the face of the rock gathers in a small pool before streaming downhill. Trees grow all around, green with small white blossoms, like snow. I don't know what they're called, in fact, I've never seen the likeness of them before. Birds sing on the branches. A huge, blue butterfly flies by.

It's... peaceful, perfect. Strangely civilized. Like I'm in a palace garden and not a Wildman's backyard.

I manage to shrug off the ruined shirt and tie it around my torso, covering my breasts, and feeling bolder, I venture a little further. A sound reaches my ears, like a bird squawking, and curious, I step past the blooming trees and—

—down the slope. I don't even have time to yelp as I roll

down, hitting stones and packed dirt, sliding in mud, for what feels like forever. A howl rolls over me, an animalistic cry of anguish and rage as I struggle to stop my fall, but whatever root I try to catch slips through my fingers. A tree looms up ahead, right in my path.

I'm going to die, I think, and that's all. I can't think past that.

Can't think at all except—*is this really how it ends?*

But a whirlwind picks me up with what strangely feels like hands and swings me out of the path of the tree—then a muscular body wraps itself around me as we hit the ground, once, twice.

Ow.

All movement stops and I remember to draw a ragged breath. A scent of spice punches me right in the chest, and I realize my face is buried in smelly furs and lift my head. I almost sneeze.

Then another realization hits me: I'm lying on top of a solid, long body, the wide ribcage underneath me rising and falling with breaths.

I lift my head a little bit more—and meet the Wildman's annoyed blue gaze. "You."

Without much ceremony, he sits up and shoves me off him. "You crazy?" he growls.

Figures that the only words he knows can be used to berate me. "What do you mean? I fell."

"This, path!"

"I slipped! I didn't know your backyard had a trap at its end!"

"Trap? No trap. *Path.*"

"Path, trap, same thing. A path that's like a slide for loggers, hidden among the trees—"

"No hidden!" His pale brows knit and his lower lip juts out like that of a whiny baby.

I snicker, because this is so ridiculous I want to roll over and laugh. "Whatever."

And that's when it hits me. He saved my life. He leaped, grabbed me as I rolled downslope and pulled me out of the way of the tree, wrapping his body around me and taking the brunt of the last tumble.

Regardless. He has just shoved me off him and called me crazy.

And I still don't know his name.

He gets to his feet and shakes his head, his long locks flying around his head. "Crazy."

"Hey, enough with the name-calling." His scent torments me, twisting me up inside, making me ache, but I won't let my body dictate my moves this time. "I'm leaving. You can't keep me here."

"No leave." He glares at me.

"You can't keep me. I'm not a pet rock or whatever pets you keep here. I'm a person. I have... friends." *If that's what I'd call my mates.* "I have a goal." *If staying alive counts.* "I'm—"

"Why leave cave?" he asks, more quietly, more... humanly.

I lift my chin. "Why not?"

"No leave. Danger."

"I was looking for you," I admit, and then I get even more annoyed because I hadn't meant to let that slip out. "Maybe. Or maybe I was just going to escape."

"I go get food." He points at some obscure point down the path.

Oh.

"Food." My stomach rumbles and I wrap my arms around me, suddenly feeling cold and weak. "I see."

"No leave cave," he goes on. "Cave is home."

"So it is your home." I'm delighted and tell myself sternly that I have no reason to be. "I mean, yeah, I get it. But it's not my home, and like I said, you can't keep me here."

"Danger," he says again, waving a hand in the air. "*Drakoryas*. Dangerous."

"Yes, you are. You are one of them, if you hadn't noticed."

A small frown forms on his face. "I am... good."

"The hell you are. You carried me away."

If he frowns any harder, his brows will dip in his eyes. "Protect."

"Protect me? From what? My own mates?" I climb to my feet warily, but anger gives me more energy than a night's sleep did. "I don't even know you! I don't even like you. You stole me away from the two men I actually had started to like!"

His eyes widen. "I stole?"

"Yes! Took me away."

"Danger. Drakoryas—"

"Enough of that." I start walking down the path, the same path I almost died on. "I'm going."

"Drakoryas eat you," he says, and I realize he's following me. Of course he is. "Take you. Kill you. Hurt you."

"Yes, yes. That's how you are, you berserkers. But you think you're different."

He falls into step beside me, grabs my elbow when my foot slips in a bit of mud. "Different, yes."

I yank my arm free and he lets go. "Why would you be any different? Why should I believe that?"

A tight, frustrated noise leaves his lips. "Parents. Parents leave... me. Here."

"Your parents left you here?"

He nods and I stop, turn to face him. "Yes."

"When?"

"Long ago. I am... little."

I try to ignore the lump forming in my throat. Finnen had said most berserkers were abandoned in the woods as children for their Fae-blood. This shouldn't come as a surprise.

"So why do you think you're different?"

"Parents..." He frowns, looks away. Seems frustrated. "Good."

"Your parents were good?"

He nods again.

"Okay..." Not sure what he's trying to tell me. "Then why did they leave you?"

He shrugs.

"If you're so good and different from other Drakoryas," I tell him quietly, "you'll take me back to my mates. *Mates.* Know this word?"

He shakes his blond, shaggy head.

"Friends?" I try. "Lovers? Or not lovers yet, but maybe one day?"

He's still frowning.

"They are good," I finally say, and his frown clears. "Good men. Take me back to them."

"Stay here," he says instead. "Danger."

And there we go, back on page one. "Gods above. I'm going. No, don't follow me."

I laugh a little at myself as I walk down the path and his steps don't follow this time. Maybe I *am* crazy. We're in the middle of nowhere, and there are other berserkers out here, maybe wild animals, too, and I don't know where I'm going. But I need to walk away, to stop my body from taking over and finding excuses for him, excuses that will allow me to sleep with him.

Or try to. He seems as receptive as my other two mates.

Just perfect. I'm a nymphomaniac in lust with three guys who won't give in to desire.

"Ariadne!" he calls out and I almost stumble at the sound of my name.

He paid attention. He saved my life. He went to find food for me.

And he also stole me from Finnen and Taj, I remind myself.

I keep walking, aware that I should stop, turn back around, talk to him. Beg him to help me. Beg him to take me back. Beg for another touch, another kiss.

Not yet, no, I won't. My pride won't let me, the same instinct of self-preservation that tells me to stop also tells me to put distance between myself and him because his blue eyes and sharp smile, his strong body and spicy scent are a hazard to my rational mind.

Just then, a big animal jumps in my path. Something cat-like. A jaguar, I think, dazed, skidding to a halt, then taking a step back. It's black and sleek with yellow eyes and big teeth. Very big teeth, curving like sabers downward.

That's not... a berserker, I think, and before I have time for anything else, I lift my hands in the second pose of Artume's moon-hunting ritual and let out a sharp cry.

The animal stills, watching me.

And the Wildman grabs me from behind, swings me over his shoulder once more and races up the path, muttering under his breath what I can only assume are curses.

Here we go again...

———

Back inside the cave, he sets me down on the furs and squats in front of me. He looks pensive. I hope he's thinking about returning me to my mates.

But no, no such chance.

"You like," he says.

"What do I like?"

"Bed." He gestures at the jumble of furs I'm sitting on. "My bed," he clarifies.

I almost laugh again. Goddess, I shouldn't. This isn't funny. "It's a bed."

"You like... soft." He runs a hand over the fur nearest to him. "Bed is soft. Like you."

"I'm soft?"

"Soft... skin?" He smiles a little, and behind the grime and thin beard, the lines of his face are harmonious and strong. Handsome.

"I'm a girl," I whisper. "So yeah, my skin is softer than yours."

"I like soft." He's gazing at me with a kind of wonder in his eyes and it makes my throat close.

I'm not a toy, I remind myself, for him to play with. Nor a pet to keep locked up in his cave.

Even if he has jaguars wandering around.

"You didn't tell me there are wild animals outside," I accuse him.

"Nature," he says, gaze still roaming over me, and shrugs. "Animals."

Right. I should have known, apparently. But I was raised inside a fort. The only animals I ever came into contact with were cats and dogs, chickens and rats, and the occasional horse. I only know jaguars from pictures.

"You stop animal," he says, his gaze returning to my face, meeting mine. "How?"

"The jaguar? I don't know." My turn to shrug. "Maybe I scared it with my cry? Or maybe you scared it, coming down the path all furry and bulky and all. You're scary."

Red touches his cheekbones. "I'm a man."

"You're a berserker!"

He shakes his head. Sits back on his heels, a mound of furs and long hair. "Who are you?"

"I'm a Temple acolyte of goddess Artume, the huntress."

"You smell... good."

So do you, I almost blurt out, but manage to keep my mouth shut.

"You okay?" He reaches out to touch my face and I flinch back. "Hurt?"

"I'm fine."

He flicks his thumb over my cheek anyway, tsks a little in the back of his throat. "I bring food," he says and is gone once more.

3

TAJ

"Why the fuck are we stopping?" Finnen snarls, his arms that are looped around my middle strangling me like a vise.

My horse nickers softly as if he's laughing at me. The gods are probably rolling on the floor by now. I've never felt so useless in my life.

"Because I've lost their trail," I snap. I lean forward in the saddle, Finnen's arms not loosening one bit, scanning the plain. "Dammit."

"I thought *I* was the blind one," he grumbles.

"It's kinda hard to follow a trail over rocks."

"I know it's rocky ground, I'm not deaf. Are we close to the hills? We're heading in that direction."

"We are. How would you know?"

He huffs, his breath ruffling the hair at the back of my neck, sending a shudder through me. "I just know."

"Come on, fess up. You have no idea."

"We're heading south," he says.

I frown. "Uh... that's true. How the fuck would you know that?"

He's stiff as a board behind me. "You mean, you can't sense the cardinal directions?"

"Me? What am I, a compass?"

He doesn't offer any other reply and I'm starting to wonder what other Fae gifts he got along with the pointy ears. What other parts of our anatomy could differ. Would his cock—?

"What do we do now, genius?" His annoyed voice makes me grin, despite the situation. "Are we going to stay here all evening?"

"We should make camp."

"She's out there! Kidnapped by a Drakoryas!"

"Think I don't know that?" I snap right back. "Gods above, Finn, I lost the fucking trail. And even I can't see in the dark."

"Then what use are you?"

"Hey, ease up with the chokehold, okay? I can't fucking breathe."

His arms relax marginally. "You should be able to feel the cardinal points."

"You think?"

"Just close your eyes," he says, "and feel the bright south of the world."

I don't even bother trying, not sure if he's being sarcastic. He still sounds pissy. "You mean, all of us with Fae blood can sense the south?"

"Not all, perhaps. I admit... my otherworldly senses have sharpened since I met Ariadne, and we all... got together."

"Fuck, why didn't I think of that?"

"Think of what? Oh, you shouldn't use your brain so much, Commander," he says. "You might strain it."

"Shut up. The *persafin*, that was the term."

"Sounds like a snake thing."

"It's a dragon thing. Dragons being the ancestors of the Fae, of course."

"Stop showing off your knowledge, and especially to a Temple priest. It's unbecoming and embarrassing."

"A renegade priest."

"As much as you are a renegade commander."

"Point is, Finn..." I rub a hand over my face, only too aware of the handsome priest's solid warm body pressed to mine from behind. "The *persafin* is a term from the old books about the Fae and their clans and it seemed to mean a pooling of power inside the clan as it came together."

"Are you saying..." He's silent for a few beats, that quicksilver mind of his surely untangling my vague words, pulling them apart and examining each one. "Pooling of power. Do you mean magic?"

"Perhaps. Or just extra sensory abilities humans don't have."

"Like sensing the south."

"Yeah."

"And... when you say it happens as the clan came together... the clan is the family."

"Composed of an omega and her or his alphas, yes."

He's silent again.

Then, with a muffled curse, he releases me, leans back and jumps off the horse. I turn around to watch him stalk through the meadow we're standing in, against the dramatic backdrop of rocky hills.

"Finn! Come back here."

He stops after a few more steps, his back to me. I watch his broad shoulders rise and fall rapidly. The knot he has tied his hair in at the back of his neck has mostly come undone, and pale strands flutter in the cold breeze.

With a sigh, I dismount, loop the reins over the horse's head and go after him. "Finn. Talk to me."

"About your inability to track Ari?"

"You know, I feel pretty damn pissed at myself right now without any help from you."

His back stiffens more. "You could always use a helping hand."

"I could, but rather in our search for Ariadne. I told you, I can't see the trail. Maybe you can help me with that."

"I'm just a blind ex-priest."

"That's bullshit and you know it." I have almost reached him by now and he hasn't moved from the spot. I take it as a good sign. "Tell me what's bothering you."

"You mean apart from failing Ariadne?"

"Yes, apart from that. Use words, Finn. Tell me."

"You want me to trust you with my innermost thoughts. To lay my feelings on the table. To act as if I've known you all my life."

"Yes," I say simply.

"Why?"

"You must know why."

This time he takes a step forward and he turns around, facing me. His blind eyes are fixed somewhere over my shoulder. "Taj..."

"Yeah?"

"Are we forming a clan?"

Ah, there is the snag, the thorn, the issue.

"Aren't we?" I ask gently, perhaps afraid myself of his answer and my own unprecedented wishes and desires.

"Damn." His jaw works. "Seriously?"

I try not to take it personally but my own jaw ticks. "That a problem for you, holy man?"

"Only if you change your mind and lead us back to the gallows."

"You know I wouldn't."

"As you said, I don't really know you. You really want me to believe you changed your mind all of a sudden and turned about to help us. Nothing comes from nothing."

"You missed the part where I fought what I felt. Like you are."

"Oh, fuck you." He chews on something he doesn't utter. Probably an insult. I wish he'd speak his mind, hash it out right now because...

Because this means something to me and it's turning my beliefs and my entire life on its head. I'm doing my fucking best to be calm about it, but it's a big mess in my head. How do I deal with it? I want to kick and punch something.

I want to grab him, wrestle him to the ground, demand... answers. Demand *more*.

But he shakes his head and stalks past me to pat the horse's rump. "Camp, then, huh?"

"For the night, yeah." Gripping the reins more tightly in my hand, I turn around to face him because I don't trust him not to leap on my horse and take off, to look for Ariadne on his own in the dark.

"Fine. And if we're forming a clan," he says stiffly, "then you should be able to sense the south. Practice, practice, Taj. Practice makes perfect."

I roll my eyes at him, and I think I catch the tail of a smirk on his handsome face, there and gone in an instant.

Damn him. Is he fucking with me? Is he just teasing me? Is he serious about all this at all or is he only interested in getting Ariadne back and leaving me behind?

Swallowing a curse of my own, I start looking for a place to camp.

———

The plain is scattered with standing rocks. It's as if a god threw his dice from the sky and they remained at odd angles, reflecting the starlight. The moon peeks out of the clouds, silvering the steep hills rising over us.

"Here is a good spot," I say.

"I'll take your word for it," Finn mutters.

"What crawled up your ass and died this time, huh?" I lead my horse to a small tree growing from a crack in the rocky ground and loop the reins over its lower branches. "You should definitely take my word, why the fuck not?"

His smirk had seemed to signify a truce but as he stalks off and stands apart, folding his muscular arms over his chest and dipping his chin, I wonder if I imagined it.

"Finn, dinner. Catch." I open one of the saddlebags and prepare to throw him a piece of jerky—then remember he can't see any of it, that I have to hand it to him myself. I clench the piece in my hand.

He says nothing.

He's an infuriating man, too stubborn, too proud, too unpredictable. Too pretty by far, damn hot in his pigheadedness. Protective and fierce.

How can anyone in their right mind not desire him? I chuckle to myself, a desperate sound. I'm mad. Mad as a march hare for wanting him and yet I can't stop.

Tomorrow. Tomorrow we'll find Ariadne, and when she's here with us, everything will make sense, somehow. Perhaps I'll wake up in my tent at the camp and find it was all a weird dream.

Do I want it to be a dream?

Why do I get a lump in my throat at the thought this might not be real?

"Hey." I turn with the intention of walking over and handing him the jerky, when I see it—a big animal running toward us through the gathering dark like a shape cut from the night.

A feline.

"Jaguar!" I shout, dropping the jerky and pulling out my knives. "Finn, get down!"

A black jaguar, sleek and deadly, picking up speed as it comes right at us, that easy feline lope that eats the distance, leaping at me—

—and Finnen is there, between me and the open jaws of the beast, using a stick—when and where did he pick it up?—as a weapon. He shoves me back and I stumble a few steps to the side, caught by surprise, as he hits the jaguar's head with the stick.

As if it's a housecat or something.

The jaguar roars and jumps on Finnen, and I find my footing, moving to grab him and thrust him behind me—but he's already grappling with the beast, the stick broken and thrown away, muscles leaping out on his arms and legs as he somehow gets the jaguar in a chokehold.

What the fuck? Who the hell is this guy?

And yeah, I know I've asked myself this question before.

Move, I tell myself. *Do something.*

Brandishing my knives, I slash at the jaguar—and the animal roars again, shaking Finnen off, sending him rolling in the dirt as I swipe with my blades at the open snout.

Finnen rolls to a crouch, braces his hands on the ground, and roars back.

A perfect imitation.

The jaguar's ears flatten, and it retreats a few steps. When Finnen launches himself at the jaguar again, before I can do more than curse him for almost giving me a heart attack, the animal turns and lopes away.

"What the fuck." I pant, staring after its dark form as it disappears in the gathering night, and turn to Finnen who's standing there, hands clenched at his sides, long hair in his face. "Gods dammit, Finn! Are you trying to get yourself killed?"

He doesn't flinch. "I was trying to save your sorry ass, idiot."

"Stop putting everyone's lives before yours, dammit! Have you ever thought maybe we don't want you dying for us?"

He tilts his head in question. "What? But—"

"Or dying at all? That maybe we want you safe and sound and not running toward death itself with your arms wide open?" I wipe my knives on my pants and sheathe them inside my boots. "Huh?"

"My arms weren't open," he mutters. Gods, he's so literal! He sounds offended. Miffed. Confused.

Terribly, inappropriately cute, dammit.

It's impossible not to kiss him.

So I don't fight it. I grab his dirty face and kiss him hard. He tastes of bitter almonds and strong black tea, of dark molasses and sexy man. He's utterly still, mouth slightly ajar as I taste him, and his eyes fall shut as I slant my head to deepen the kiss.

Then he jerks back. Stills again.

"Okay?" I whisper.

"Oh..." He looks dazed. Blinks. "But Ari..."

"If we are a clan," I say firmly, "then you need to know how much I want you, too."

"But... this clan..."

"Alphas don't have to have sex with one another, I'll give you that. But I want you. And it feels right. Don't you want it?" I rub a hand over my eyes, rephrase. "Don't you want *me*? As in, have sex with me? You know, the undressed, sweaty kind, though I don't know if there's any other kind of—"

"I'm still not sure about this clan business," Finnen says.

And something hot flares inside me. "Seriously? That's all you got to say? Listen. If anyone is qualified for this shit, it's you."

"This *shit*?"

"Yeah. You're a priest. You were raised to believe in the extraordinary. The magic, the divine, the miracles. Fate. I was raised to be practical, believe in my own two hands and my daring to make it through the day. If anyone should believe that these bonds, this clan, this *persafin* is possible, it should be you, not me."

"There you go, whining again," he mutters but he looks thoughtful.

Then again, he might just be pissed. Hard to tell with Finnen. Maybe even he himself can't tell the difference anymore.

"You are the one who started this," I say. "You and Ariadne."

"And there you go again, talking about what happened like it's a mistake."

"No, dammit, that's not what I mean. I mean that... that you started something and now you say you're not sure about it. About this *business*. That's what you said. You think you're the only one furious because your plans for the future have been turned upside down?"

"I'm not furious," he says quietly.

"Come again?"

"I never cared much about the future. I did my best to fit in, but it isn't... it wasn't what I wanted."

"So what do you want?"

A shrug. A flush on high cheekbones. "Nothing," he says and brushes by me, to go the gods know where.

"We all want something," I counter, turning and grabbing his arm, forcing him to stop and face me once more.

"Speak for yourself," he breathes, but his flush remains. "Let go of me."

I release him after a long moment and he staggers away from me, walking backward, uncharacteristically awkward.

Then he stumbles.

"The fuck, Finn." I catch him before he crashes into the rocks. "Finn!"

He growls. "Get your hands off me. I just..."

"Finn..."

A raw sound escapes him. Instead of pushing me away, he grabs at my arms, steps right into my embrace.

This time when I kiss him, he kisses me back, falling into me, and a knot unravels in my chest.

We haven't found Ariadne yet, but this clan has begun knitting itself together. I hold him in my arms, marveling at this feeling. It's like holding a star that fell from the sky, vibrating with power in my embrace, and I wonder.

I wonder what will happen when we find her, if she will draw more alphas to her, if I'll want them the way I want Finnen. The way I want her.

"We should sleep," I say. "So we can get up at first light to resume our search."

He pulls back. Nods. Looks strangely subdued, which makes me worry that he's in worse shape than he cares to show me.

"Sleep," I tell him. "I'll take first watch."

4

ARIADNE

This time I don't move from the spot, curled up on the furs, cataloging my new cuts and bruises from my tumble down the slope.

I'm okay, at least that's true. Nothing worse has happened, unless you count the fact that every time I touch him or he touches me, the ache in my belly recedes and then returns, making me grit my teeth.

What should I do?

Keep talking to him, I tell myself. *Get him to relax. To like you, trust you. Then tell him again to take you back.*

But back where? Finnen and Taj won't stay where I left them indefinitely. In fact, if my hunch is correct, they're tracking us, so only the gods know where they are right now.

What do I do?

I drag my fingers through my bedraggled hair. I need a wash. And a comb. And clean clothes.

And so does he, I think when he enters the cave a while later, carrying two skinned hares. He glances at me, his shoulders relaxing—he had been afraid I'd leave again, I realize

—and then sits at the entrance and quickly starts a fire with a flint and a stone.

By the time he has stuck a spit through the hares and has them roasting over the low fire, I go to sit beside him. His eyes track my movements. He says nothing as I sit on a protuberance in the rock. With a small stick, he pokes at the burning wood.

"I need a wash," I say.

His eyes narrow.

"As do you," I continue. "Let me cut your hair, shave your beard. Wash you."

"Wash?"

"Wash."

He seems to be considering my offer. "Wash? With water?"

"Yes, with water. That's how you wash."

"Wash hands," he says.

"And body. And hair. And face."

Another narrow look. "Why?"

"Why not? If I'm stuck here for now, might as well get comfortable, and you could use a wash and trim, if only to check if you really are human, as you claim."

He doesn't rise to the bait, still nailing me with that sharp gaze. "Not run away?"

"I won't," I mutter.

That's not really a promise, is it? I haven't sworn on any god or goddess that I won't try to escape. This is just conversation.

That's falling low, a voice whispers in my mind. *Twisting logic and ethics to fit your actions. Then again, who's in the wrong here? Ethics is already twisted, and none of this makes any rational sense.*

Besides, I still don't know where I could run to.

And maybe, just maybe, all I want is a chance to see his body underneath all those furs, see his face under all that hair, and prove to myself that he's not as desirable as my body seems to believe.

One can only hope...

The water running down the wall of the cave and the small pool are perfect for washing ourselves, apart from a small detail: the water is so cold my hand is instantly numb the moment I plunge it inside.

The Wildman is watching me, crouched down beside the pool, a calculating look in his blue eyes. He's like one of the Temple cats, waiting for a chance to jump on a hanging rope or piece of cloth to bat it around. Waiting to play.

It sends a shiver down my spine.

"You wouldn't happen to have scissors?" I nod at the cave entrance. "If not, a sharp blade will do."

"Blade," he repeats.

"A knife. To cut your hair and beard."

He shifts a little, takes out a sharp-looking knife from under the furs, and I have to wonder where he sheaths it.

He holds it out and after a moment's hesitation, I take it. "You wash," he says.

"I will help you wash. Come on." I beckon with the knife. "Get in here."

Maybe that's a mistake—flashing that bright blade around —because he shakes his head. "You first."

"Oh, come on. I need to cut your hair, work on your beard. I'll get sweaty and full of hairs. I'll wash afterward."

"You." He doesn't even get up from his crouch. A smirk tugs at his mouth. "Go first."

"You don't trust me?"

The smirk becomes more pronounced, more savage, showing a bit of fang.

Crap.

"Fine, I'll go first. Big baby. Afraid of cold water, are you?" I place the knife down on the ground by the pool and turn my back to him to undress. I mean, he's seen my breasts, touched them, but I feel strangely uneasy. It's due to my Temple upbringing, probably, and to having chaste Artume as my goddess.

Worst goddess choice ever for an omega whose mind is currently stuck on sex, but there you have it.

I undo the knot I made behind my back to keep the torn shirt from falling, take it off and place it by the knife on the ground, then undo the laces keeping my woolen pants up. I bend to free my dirty bare feet from the fabric, pile everything up, and turn to step into the pool.

I yelp.

Oh, goddess. So cold. My teeth start to chatter and numbness travels up my legs after the first shock. My nipples tighten, my belly muscles clench. It's like liquid ice.

And another yelp escapes me when I find myself face to face—okay, face to chest—with the Wildman who is no longer crouching but standing by the pool, staring at me.

At my breasts, to be more precise, and the rest of me. His cheekbones are pink, eyes dark, lips parted.

He looks as if he desires me, and I remember how hard he was when he'd lain over me inside the cave, but there's no way to really tell with the amount of furs hanging off his frame. It's like he's inside a furry ball, bundled up like the old priests in winter.

Just wash yourself, Ari, get it over with, before your feet freeze and fall off. Let the berserker look to his heart's content. If he's not interested in more than some voyeurism, then who cares?

I turn away, not to see that look in his eyes, not to wonder, because the ache in my belly is only temporarily numbed by the cold. Cupping my hands under the trickling water, I wash myself as quickly as humanly possible, scrubbing with my hands to get the dirt off my skin. I throw water over my head, wetting my hair, scrubbing at my scalp.

So frigging cold...

Then he's again in front of me, having gone around the pool, muttering something under his breath, one hand under his furs, moving back and forth.

Before I can react to that, he starts to undress—which means that he starts to pull his furs off, one by one. There seems to be a piece going around his neck, then another over his shoulders, then one around his torso, and another around his waist. So many pieces, falling off him one by one. I'm too entranced by this slow reveal of him that I stand in the icy water, just staring at his lithe but sculpted body as it finally becomes visible, not as bulky as it had seemed with all the furs heaped on him, but rather sinuous and yet muscular. More muscular than Finnen and Taj, I think, but not by much, and under the filth he seems to be very fair.

He kicks off his short boots before he's done undressing, though by now he's only clad in a sort of leather loincloth that nly covers his crotch and winds around his hips to keep it in ace. Can't help but notice the huge bulge in it, though, a tent t means his cock is hard.

Very hard and very large, and I swallow, unable to look

shoots me a determined look and reaches for the knot g the loincloth in place. He's about to join me in the pool lly doubt we'll get any cleaning done. I'm sure washing his mind right now, and I'm back in the *oh yes* and *oh* een phase of earlier, torn between my body's desires nd's worries.

wrinkles. There's a smell of burnt on the air, burnt

ifferent growl echoes against the rocks, and he e entrance of the cave.

reakfast is burning over the flames.

meat off the flames and throws it on the

ground. The meat has burnt together with the spit and the sticks he had planted into the soil to support the spit.

"Maybe the inside is edible?" I hazard, stepping out of the pool, my hands over my breasts. "Leave it to cool down and we can check."

He's staring down at the meat like it has betrayed him personally, a pout on his face that makes me want to giggle. He looks so much like a little boy whose toy broke. And I feel him because I'm starving.

"You don't have any other food, huh? You never save food for a rainy day?"

"Squirrels save," he mutters. "Ants save."

"That's a no, then?"

"I have some apples," he says. "But I want meat."

"Me too. Maybe we'll be able to have it later. Come." J toward the pool. "Shaving time."

Time to take a look at the rest of him.

———

To be honest, I don't expect him to sit and I want with him, but that's what he does. He of a shock at finding the meat burning Surely it must have happened to him b to everyone who cooks?

He's so distracted, he doesn't ev his loincloth and his gaze is dista on the ground by the pool or distance as I pull my pants b torso before picking up the

"Ready?" Not waiting kneel behind him. The pale blue, the cloud.

"Sure you don't mind losr

He grunts when I gather his tangled, grimy locks in one hand, weighing them. It doesn't sound like an answer, more like a "go away, don't bother me" grunt, but he doesn't shove me away or get up to leave, and I choose to take it as an invitation.

After all, what do I need an invitation for? He's my nameless captor. He's the beast who caught me. I'm about to do him a favor and turn him back into a human.

Just like magic.

Let's see if it works.

Carefully, I start cutting off his locks. I keep the length uniform at chin level because I'm not sure I won't botch it completely if I cut it shorter. You can fix longer hair, but short hair? Hard to do. My tongue sticking out between my lips, I cut and cut, tangled, gray locks falling all around him.

At some point, he seems to wake up from whatever trance he's fallen into and turns his head to look at me, though thankfully he does it slowly or I'd have cut off the tip of his ear.

"What... what are you doing?"

"Cutting your hair," I say cheerfully. "Remember? And hey, that was a full question. No missing words. Good job. Maybe language is coming back to you." I lower the knife. "The beard now."

"I remember..." He frowns, raises a hand to touch the much shorter locks. "Remember the past. I don't talk... to many people."

"Makes sense. You're in the middle of nowhere, surrounded by jaguars and the gods know what else." I get up and walk around to crouch in front of him. "Sit still now. Just going to trim your beard."

Those wide blue eyes blink at me.

I hack at his scraggly beard kind of haphazardly until the shape of his jaw shows through, square and strong. His beard is blond under the filth and so is his hair. I wonder what the real color is once it's washed. I cut off as much facial hair as I dare without risking injury to his face, and put the knife down.

And then I take my first real look at him and almost fall on my ass in shock.

Holy smokes.

Wow.

Without the tangled bush of hair around his face, the exotic uptilt of his blue eyes is even more prominent, as are his high cheekbones and the strong lines of his face, and his mouth... it's firm, very masculine, and yet it looks soft and full as he gazes blankly back at me.

Still kind of lost inside his head.

"Did something spook you?" I frown at him and resist the urge to stroke my fingertips over his lips, over his jaw. "I don't even know what's normal for you. But who cares? Come on, time to wash."

Of course he doesn't move, so with a sigh, I cup water in my hands and pour it over his head, watch the dirt run from his locks down his body.

That finally seems to jerk him awake and he grows, grabbing my wrists, baring his teeth at me. "What?" he snarls.

I bare my teeth right back. "Washing."

"We wash together," he says, jumping to his feet, and dragging me with him into the pool. "And call me Kiaran."

5

ARIADNE

Kiaran.

That's his name.

I gasp and flail as he pulls me into the frigid water, but when his warm body collides with mine, I feel heat ignite inside me. A fire, erasing the cold. He hauls me against him and his scent is a punch to my senses, making me drunk and dizzy.

This is my mate. His scent is perfect, his body magnificent, his face gorgeous, his gaze scorching.

The ears poking through the pale locks are slightly pointed, I notice, and for some reason, that makes me smile. We're Fae blood, and that might explain the scraggly beard. Fae don't grow full beards. The signs are there indeed.

"Kiaran," I whisper and rise on tiptoe to kiss him, finally giving in to my body's needs, to the fierce attraction, the gut-wrenching pull of him. His arms around me are firm, powerful, his cock thick and hard under the leather loincloth, trapped between us. I run my hands over his hard pecs, his muscular shoulders and biceps, and a groan rumbles up his chest.

"Ariadne," he breathes and bows his head to kiss me. But a

roar shakes the air, coming from the plain below, and his head snaps back up. "Jaguar."

"Shit. No, Kiaran—"

All air leaves my lungs when he lifts me in his arms and steps out of the pool, striding toward the cave entrance. "Protect you."

"Great, we're back to one-word sentences. But—"

"Jaguar," he says, ducking to clear the low lintel of the entrance and carrying me into the cave. "Danger."

"Okay. Can we barricade the door with something? Until it goes away?"

"I hunt jaguar. Punch." He puts me down on his makeshift bed of furs and demonstrates with his fist.

I almost snicker, it's cute, though I'm sure he packs a mean punch. "Punch the jaguar in the face?"

A grin tugs at his full lips. "In the face."

"Or you can close the door," I whisper, touching his face. "And stay with me."

A grunt leaves his lips. He turns his face into my touch, pale lashes lowering over blue eyes. "To protect?"

"Among other things."

His bare, muscular body slides over mine, pressing down, his hot length pressing between my legs, and I need him. I need him to lose that stupid loincloth and bury himself inside of me.

He dips his head, taking my mouth, brutally kissing me. It's more like a claim, a declaration of war than a kiss, a hunger that he doesn't know how to appease, and something in me answers.

Finally, finally.

I arch up against him, loop my arms around his neck, kiss him back. His taste floods my senses, his scent and the feel of his taut flesh against mine wreaking havoc with my thoughts.

He pulls back suddenly, groaning, reaching down between us to press on his cock through the leather. "Feels good..."

"Yes," I agree fervently.

Then his hand presses between my bare legs and I gasp. "Wet..."

"Yes." I'm so wet for him. I moan when he pushes one finger inside me, strokes deep. "Yes..."

"Fuck," he breathes and I don't know if he's cursing or suggesting we fuck, or just naming the act of what we're doing or are about to do—and oh my stars, he's added a second finger, I think, and I'm about to come apart—

With a deep growl, he withdraws his fingers, causing me to cry out, and then scoots back and buries his face between my legs.

Oh, dear Goddess.

I tense as an assault as brutal as his kiss is unleashed. He rubs his bristly cheeks and chin against my wet folds, licks me and stabs into me with his tongue, tortures my nub and sucks on it, until I can't draw breath.

Until I shatter, moaning loudly as the pressure in me breaks and pleasure washes me away like a flood and I'm drowning in a sea of stars.

Oh...

I blink up at the ceiling of the cave, stunned.

After an endless moment, I find his face over me, his blue eyes amused. "Good?"

"Good," I whisper, my voice a croak. "So, so good."

He grins, and oh boy. He's mouth-wateringly pretty when he grins, his sharp cheekbones flushed. His sky-blue eyes are fringed by long lashes, the now chin-length locks brush his neck, and the broad shoulders magnificently muscled.

I reach for him with a small moan, needing to trace the lines of his face, his lips that are glistening with my wetness, my pleasure. I tug his head down until I can kiss him, taste myself on his mouth, and his lashes lower, a groan rumbling through him.

I don't know who this girl is, moaning and writhing on the furs in a Wildman's cave, begging to be fucked. When was it that I served Artume and read her scriptures, bowed to her statue and didn't touch anyone, ever, not even my own body?

This time when he pulls back, I reach between us, find his cock so hard it's peeking out from the top of the loincloth. When I touch it, he shudders. His eyes lift to meet mine, dark and dazed with lust.

I tug on his loincloth, freeing more of his hard length, until I can wrap my fingers around it. It's so thick they can't close, can't encircle it fully.

It's my first time gripping a man's erection and it's a heady feeling, both strange and arousing. My belly clenches painfully, but I ignore it, fascinated by the look on Kiaran's face.

Eyes half-closed, lips parted, a tension in his body making muscles leap out in harsh relief in his chest and arms. He has one hand planted by my head, the other by his side as he half-turns to gaze down where I'm holding him, literally in the palm of my hand, his cock throbbing, swelling more, forcing my fingers to open more.

I squeeze a little, hunting for a reaction, and he thrusts into my hand, a whine leaving his throat. It takes my breath away. He does it again, and again, fluid seeping from the head of his cock, coating my fingers, making my hold slippery. He's wet, too, I think, wet and hard for me, and my core flutters and pulses.

The next time he does it, he gasps, and I feel his cock jerk a little in my hand. He's close, I think, he's as unused to this as I am, he likes it, he wants it, he's going to come—

With a snarl, he rips my fingers away from his hard-on and takes things into his own hands. I don't have time to react as he hunches over me, teeth peeled back, brows drawn together.

Grabbing his cock in a big fist and jacking off savagely,

violently taking his pleasure, perhaps in the only way he knows.

Then shuddering and pressing his hard cock down between us, his hips rocking as his hard length slides against my belly, then higher, between my breasts, leaving hot smears of his need on my skin.

Finally spilling all over my breasts and belly, sticky ropes of white cum, marking me.

It makes me shudder with pleasure, even if it's a token marking, temporary, not there to stay. Even if this isn't the sex I need to curb the heat consuming me little by little. It's barely enough to ease the pain in my belly, to make me feel languid and limp, legs tangled in the furs, the Wildman's muscular body starting to weigh down on me as he finishes off and the tension leaves him.

He catches himself on both hands before he smothers me. His eyes are heavy-lidded as he gazes down at me, the blue turned to black in the dimness, and he looks like an old god, a companion to Artume on her hunts, wild and golden, dark and bright, mysterious and yet naïve like a child, and...

Oh, Goddess. What about Finnen? What about Taj?

Guilt pelts me. I turn my face away.

His warm breath is on my hair, then on my neck, followed by his lips, and my body arches of its own volition, shivering in need and pleasure.

I should trust my body to know what is good for it, what will take the pain away, replace it with pleasure, give into its demands and drag Kiaran back down, guide his cock between my legs where I'm starting to ache once more. His mouth there was amazing, fantastic, but it's not what will fix my problem, what will give my body what it craves.

Wait a moment... I frown and plant a hand on Kiaran's naked, muscled chest. Trust my body? The world is full of stories of women who did just that and their tragic ends. Women who don't think are used and discarded and left to deal with the consequences while men usually just move on with their lives, unaffected.

I turn to glare at him, annoyed at him though I know perfectly well that I haven't resisted his advances, in fact I have made advances on him, and the sight of his handsome face, still slack with pleasure, sends a bolt through me. It feels like a touch of lightning, shooting through my body, wrenching a gasp from my throat.

I *want*. Before I know it, my other hand has curled around his neck, and I lift my hips to press against his still semi-hard cock that's now nestled between them.

So good... Need this... Need him...

Gods, how can you battle a desire so fierce it won't let you frigging think?

He seems to be lost in the same bottomless well of arousal as me, because his gaze moves to my mouth and he brushes his lips over mine, more gently this time, tentatively, as if testing something. His tongue drags over my lips, rough like a cat's, and I moan, clutching at him. When his tongue plunges into my mouth, mine dances against it, and I almost come just from that.

Holy virgin goddess, do you have any idea what you're missing? And this isn't even proper sex. Will having him inside of me feel better than this? Than his mouth or his fingers? My body says, how can you doubt it? It will fix everything, better everything, connect all the dots and the world will make sense once you've been fucked within an inch of your life by these men, all these men and their big hard dicks.

But, a small voice protests timidly somewhere at the back of my mind, *will it? What if it doesn't?*

I break the kiss, even as I scoff at my own doubts. *I'm an omega. Of course it will. It's what I need, what going into heat is all about.*

Babies, the voice continues. My own damn voice. *And that's what you want just as the Empire has decided to hunt you all down and kill you, right? All of you Fae-blood.*

Shit.

Exactly. *Holy shit.*

"Ariadne." He speaks my name again and he draws it out, making it sound like a prayer or a story. Then he makes it a question. "Ariadne?"

Right. We had been kissing. And... pleasuring each other. And then I stopped.

Because of doubts. And guilt. And *logic*.

While I'm still clutching at him, my body desperate to continue, desperate—

A strange roar echoes outside the cave, more distant than before, thankfully, but he jerks back.

"Jaguar. Hunt."

"What do you mean? It's hunting?"

He nods. "I am going."

"No, Kiaran. You're not going to fight the beast, okay?" I grab at his arms as he starts lifting himself off me. "Stay with me. Kiaran—"

"Jaguar hunting *people*." He pulls away from me effortlessly, not even seeming to notice the death grip I had on his arms, and pulls his loincloth up. "I can't allow it."

"People." I blink. "Whoa, what? How would you know that? Maybe it's hunting deer or... or I don't know, hares and foxes."

"People," he says. "I know that roar."

"You do? But..." I scramble to my feet as he starts toward the cave entrance. "Wait! I'm coming with you."

He shoots me a glare over one big shoulder. "No, you're not."

"Try and stop me."

He stops and glares some more. "I'll tie you to the bed."

"You can't. You don't have a bedpost."

"I'll tie you up and leave you on the bed." He starts toward me, the darkness in his gaze telling me he means it. He will do anything to stop me.

To protect me.

And he's about to go out there and fight a jaguar to help people.

Another roar interrupts him. It seems to be closer now. Distracted, he glances back at the entrance.

"Are you going to kill the jaguar?"

"Stay here," he commands me again and stalks off, starting to run before he even steps out of the cave.

And I run after him.

Who is this man? Living in a cave like a savage hermit, seeming so innocent and yet so definitely a man, strong and tough and sexy. Selfless and brave. He said he carried me away to save me from the other Drakoryas. He didn't know I was with anyone else. He's been reluctant to let me out in case I'm attacked.

He makes my heart hammer in the same way Finnen and Taj do, just like his body makes mine sing.

They are nice men. Nice, sexy, muscular men who smell like my favorite dessert, but what does it matter if they're nice or sexy and how they smell? I should be running away from them.

Maybe this is my chance to make my escape.

6

FINNEN

"I thought you were keeping first watch," I snap.

"I was."

"Then what's the fucking jaguar doing back here?"

"Can't be sure it's the same one," Taj mutters, grabbing my arm and hauling me back two steps. "Stay here."

"The fuck you say."

"Come on, Finn. Do as I say for once, will you? Let me deal with it."

The beast growls, a low sound that makes my hackles rise. "You can't find your own ass without my help."

A soft snort. "And why are you thinking about my ass now, priest?"

"Dammit, Taj, I'm not joking! Just—"

The jaguar roars, and before I can find my wits, Taj shoves me backward, sends me staggering into a goddamn bush.

"Fuck you," I snarl, disentangling myself from the thorny branches and stumbling wildly in a circle, lifting my hands, dizzy and disoriented. "What the hell. Where—?"

There's a yowl and a thump and my fucking heart drops. "Taj? Fuck, Taj, where are you, you—"

"Here. I'm here." His hand clamps on my arm again and hauls me back a few steps. "I wounded the animal, stay out of the way."

"Fucking hell, it's going to attack, what the fuck did you do?"

"Hey, relax, my grumpy friend. It attacked us first. I was only defending us."

"Then you should have fucking killed it and stopped playing around!"

"Damn, someone's snappy today," he mutters. "Did you miss breakfast?"

I almost punch him, or would have if I wasn't too panicky to focus on his voice.

I'm unnerved. In the dark, as I always am, on a plain where I've never been, facing an animal I've never seen.

Yes, I'm snappy and grumpy. I'm fucking terrified, not that I'll ever admit as much to Taj if it kills me. My heart is stabbing at my ribs with every beat.

And then Taj pushes me back again and I lose what little fucking composure I have left.

"Where? Where the fuck is it?" I catch myself before I fall and turn back toward him. "Taj, damn you!"

He's racing away from me. To draw the jaguar away from me, my rational mind tells me, but I'm way too pissed with him, way too scared for him to listen to that little voice, the voice that tells me that I should stay put, let him draw the animal away, that I can't see, therefore I'm justified to let him help me, let him protect me.

Fuck that shit. I'm the one who should protect the idiot. Fighting battles with the army—if that, because we haven't had a real war in a thousand years—doesn't compare to fighting jaguars one-on-one.

And what experience do you *have fighting wild beasts?* the little voice screams in my head, but this time I ignore it. Taj is running, and I hear the jaguar leaping after him, and damn reason and self-preservation, I'm not letting anyone take Taj from me.

From us.

I start running blindly toward the animal, yelling a war-cry —and the shape of the jaguar erupts into light.

It takes me a long moment to realize what I am seeing, to realize that I *am* seeing something, almost a moment too long, and I lurch to a stop, trying to make sense of what my senses are showing me.

The jaguar turns and leaps at me without breaking stride— a new target, a new annoying meal on two legs—and its shape is outlined against the dark world, a lightning strike in the shape of an attacking predator, claws extended, jaw open.

I leap, too, to meet it halfway, barely registering Taj's howl of dismay. I twist my body in midair, bringing my fists down on the jaguar's huge head, still howling out my anger and my damn outrage at the world.

This fucking world.

Next thing I know I'm lying on my ass in the dirt, my head ringing and my chest hurting like a bitch, and I can't fucking remember where I am and why I taste blood in my mouth.

Light flashes against the dark, again and again, keeping time with my heart. My head pounds sickly.

Then a hand grasps mine, slippery with blood. The coppery scent makes me want to throw up.

"Finnen? Finn!" Taj sounds kind of frantic. "Are you all right?"

"Fine," I grunt. "I'm fine." He pulls me up to sit and I bow my head, hoping the sickness passes. "Yours?" I growl. "Is the blood yours?"

"No. It's the jaguar's."

"Is it dead? Did you kill it?"

"No, it... got dealt with."

"What in the nine hells do you mean?" I mutter, lifting my other hand to press against my temple with a wince. I'm still sitting on my ass and I don't even know if the jaguar is dead. "Use actual words, Taj, and tell me."

"Calm your tits."

"How can I calm my—?"

"Someone else took care of it for us."

"If you don't explain, Taj, and quickly, I might just kill you."

He laughs, a breathless sound. "Now you're making me hard, priest."

Gods give me strength. "Speak, will you?"

"It's a Drakoryas. He killed the beast."

"A Drakoryas," I whisper, blinking at nothing. I have a feeling about this. Not necessarily a bad one, but a strong feeling nonetheless. "Where is he? Did you let him go?"

"Excuse me, asshole, for wanting to check first if you're still alive."

"Get him." I clasp his hand and use it to haul myself to my feet. I weave dizzily. "Go get him!"

When he lets go, I almost go back down. Stumbling drunkenly, I follow the sounds, the lights having gone out already. Only during fighting and sex, I think and I want to laugh—or throw up, because more and more clues to my Fae nature are piling up.

The Drakoryas roars and Taj swears and I stagger toward them.

"Taj! Talk to me." I hold one arm outstretched in front of me, as I was taught as a child to walk the rooms of our house. As if it can help me out here. "Taj, dammit!"

"Look what I got you, honey," Taj drawls, a savage grin shaping his voice. "A honeymoon present. He bites a little but is otherwise quite cute."

"You're an idiot," I say absently, following the thread of his voice.

"Where is the pat on my head?" Taj says. "Won't you tell me I'm a good boy for fetching him so quickly?"

I swallow a sigh and find to my consternation that I want to laugh. "Damn you, Taj."

"Yeah, yeah, you said that before," he grunts.

The Drakoryas growls but no sounds of scuffle reach me. "Got him?"

"He's not fighting me," he says, confirming my suspicions.

I step closer and closer, the Wildman's low growl directing me to him.

I grab him by the neck and hear Taj's startled hiss. "Aren't you the one who took our girl, Wildman?"

"You think he's the one?" Taj mutters.

"I doubt there are many Drakoryas in each territory and he can't have taken her far."

"Ariadne," the Wildman breathes.

"That's right." I feel another growl rising in my throat. "She talked to you."

"Talk. Yes."

"You know Ariadne? You..." Taj sounds like he's about to explode with rage. "You're the one who stole her from us? I'm going to fucking kill you."

Oh Gods.

"Wait. Taj, just wait!" With my one free hand, I reach for him, grab him.

"What?" he snarls. "Let me hurt him."

"He knows this place. Knows where she is."

"Ariadne," the Wildman says again and I wish I could see his face, his expression, read what the sound of her name means to him. It almost sounds like longing—which is another word for lust, I tell myself, and why wouldn't he want her?

"Take us to her," I growl and shove him forward, some distant part of me wondering why he isn't fighting us, in fact why he saved us and why the fuck he smells like a cake.

This isn't fucking confusing at all.

Especially when something sweet spills in the air and I lift my head to follow its trail.

Ari...

It smells like her.

7

ARIADNE

How can you be crying as you run away from your kidnapper, feeling as if your heart is breaking in two? How can you be torn apart because you need to find your other two mates, make sure they're okay and throw your arms around them again—but you also want to stay?

How is this my life, going from the lonely quiet of the Temple to running through the wilderness, breathless with fear? Going from utter need to utter release, from utter fear to utter connection, from joy to affection to love—

No, stop this, Ari. This isn't love.

Don't let your body command you.

A bit late for that, isn't it?

What happens when I go into full heat? What will happen to me? What will happen to my mates?

What do I want?

It's never seemed more complicated.

Blinded by tears, I have to stop and wipe the wetness from my eyes, struggle to catch my breath.

In the distance, the jaguar roars again.

And now I'm worried about Kiaran.

I press the heels of my palms into my eyes, groaning. How is this possible? I barely know him.

Then again, I barely knew Finnen and Taj a few days ago.

What is this madness?

"Kiaran?" I turn in a slow circle. The trees are closing in on me. The silence is heavy and ominous. "Kiaran!"

If there is one jaguar, could there be more?

Do jaguars run in packs? Do they have... nests? Is there a mamma jaguar around here, waiting to pounce on me? I'm not very far from the cave, given I can find my way back. I think I can. Maybe I should have obeyed Kiaran and stayed there.

But I can't give up on Finnen and Taj.

Damn.

What I should do is try to get to a high place, see if I catch a glimpse of them.

And it's still a shock that by that I mean the three of them.

Although deep inside I know, after smelling him, after touching him, after kissing him, that Kiaran is one of my fated mates, too.

———

I fail to find the way back up to the cave—because that's a high point, and if I hadn't been so intent on escaping I might have thought of seeking a vantage point to scan the area. After all, I need to know where I am and which way to go.

Away from the Summer Capital. But also not back to the fort of Artare.

Where can a runaway Fae-blooded omega about to go into heat run to?

What am I going to do?

Fighting despair, I walk further, looking for a way up, trying to catch a glimpse of Kiaran, or maybe a sign from the gods.

"Artume!" I yell, stumbling among the trees. "I served you for so long. Won't you speak to me?"

But she never has. Why should she start now?

"Artume!"

Her name returns in echoes, mocking me.

I scream in frustration, my voice bouncing. "Answer me!"

But she doesn't.

It's becoming painfully clear that I'm lost. Hopelessly lost. The trees all look the same, the faint animal trails repeating themselves in an endless loop, sending me round and round through the woods, or so it feels like. Impossible to tell without a landmark, without knowing which way I came from and which way I'm going.

Much like my life right now, and the gods love a good metaphor, don't they? As well as good punishments and blood.

Blood. I stop, glance down. A cut on my leg is sluggishly bleeding. And then I think I see patterns flashing on my hands. I stare at them, mystified.

What's happening?

"I need to find them!" I call out to the trees, the clouds, the skies. "Help me! Why won't you ever help me? Up there, in your crystal spheres of cloud and rain, mighty and useless! Help me! Help—" A branch hits me in the face, leaving a long burning scratch on my cheek. "By the dragons of old!"

Wait.

The unnamed god. He spoke to me, the only god who ever has.

'*Sidde Drakai,*' he'd said. '*Drakai evenen.*'

Whatever that means.

So I should dance for him. My head is buzzing, spinning, and I feel a pain in my ribs, a pain in my arm. Phantom pains.

I picture the god's statue. I lift my hands in supplication, bow my head and whisper words of prayer, words of respect.

"Hear me, *Sidde Drakai*, if that is your name. I danced for you at the Temple, against all the rules, and I was cast out. Hear me now and guide me. Help me find my mates."

I spread my hands, bow from the waist, slide one foot to the side, bend my knees. It's a new dance, one I have never danced before, a dance I'm offering since I have nothing else.

Movement and faith.

"Please, Old One. Help."

'Drakai,' the deep, resonant voice whispers inside my head and I gasp, dropping my arms to my sides. 'Drakai inassa. Drakai inonen.'

More mysterious words, but the voice sounds benevolent, as if the god is somehow pleased.

"Please," I whisper again, "please—"

And then I smell them.

All three of them.

Although the pain in my belly hits like a sledgehammer, I start walking again, trying to follow that trail, which proves harder than it sounds. I'm not a hound. I've never done more than follow my nose to the kitchens of the fort on occasion, but I keep moving, holding on to my faith in the god's help, to the reality of their scents, like a somnambulist following the thread of a dream, afraid I'll wake up and lose my grip on what's real.

That's when I hear them.

I hear Finnen's voice, calling out my name, I hear Taj yelling for me and warmth spills inside my chest.

What about Kiaran? Has something happened to him? Why is he silent?

I draw a shaky breath, hardly able to believe it, a startled laugh escaping me. "I'm here! I'm here, please..."

And I start to run, stumbling over roots and brambles, down the slight slope, prepared to come face-to-face with an enraged jaguar at every turn, the symbols flashing on my hands seeming to dance around me, glancing off the tree boles and the grass.

"Ari!" It's Taj who appears first, racing toward me, dark hair flying, a grin on his face, and this time I laugh out long and loud, because Finnen is following more slowly, a hand clamped on Kiaran's arm, the two of them like twins with their pale long hair and pale faces.

I fall to my knees and bow over, still laughing, tears slipping down my cheeks.

'Drakai inassa. Drakai inonen.'

Thank you, God of the dragons.

———

Taj has lifted me in his arms and I'm shamelessly clinging to his strong neck and shoulders, my face buried against the scratchy fabric of his shirt. Finnen and Kiaran are following us and I want to touch them, but I'm wrung out like a wet rag, relief mingling with exhaustion to sap all strength from my limbs.

"Are you all right?" Taj asks me, and I feel his voice rumble through him as much as hear it, a touch as much as it is a sound.

"I'm okay." And then I remember something. "You should put me down. You're hurt."

"You mean, he hurt me. Your Wildman."

"To be fair," Finnen says, and the sound of his deep voice makes me shiver pleasantly, "you attacked him first."

"I thought he was going to hurt you both."

"No hurt," Kiaran says, and his voice is a caress over my skin.

"See?" I murmur.

"I'll be damned. He can string words together." Taj huffs.

"And he has a name," I say. "Kiaran."

"Well, how was I supposed to know, huh?" Taj's strides slow. "It's starting to get dark. We should find a spot for the night."

I lift my head, searching for my other two mates. "Maybe

Kiaran knows a safe place for the night?" And I almost fall out of Taj's arms. "Finn! What's the matter with him? Kiaran?"

Kiaran has one arm around my priest and Finn is leaning heavily against him. "Hit his head. Dizzy."

And Finnen's silence is all the confirmation I need.

"Put me down," I tell Taj and this time he obeys, probably hearing in my voice that I really mean it. The moment my feet hit the ground, I all but run to Finnen, touch his face. He has a crust of blood coating one side of his face. "What happened?"

"He hit the jaguar and the jaguar didn't appreciate it," Taj mutters by way of explanation, "so it threw him down, kinda hard. Your Wildman and I finished the beast off before it decided to have him for dinner."

"It's not funny," I whisper, worry turning my stomach into a rock. "How bad is it, Finn?"

"I'll live," he says and places his hand over mine on his cheek. "Are you going to ask me if I see double?"

"Now *this* is funny," Taj says.

I roll my eyes. "Are you nauseous? And I'm asking Finn, not you, Taj."

"Ouch," Taj mutters.

"I'm better now," Finnen says, and I wish I could believe him, the stubborn idiot.

"You know hits on the head are tricky."

"This might shock you, acolyte, but I, too, received the standard Temple education, including health lore."

"Okay, he sounds like his normal self. He'll be fine." I turn to Taj. "Come help Finn so that Kiaran can find us shelter for the night."

There's a moment of frozen silence, frozen time, where we all contemplate the fact that I've taken over the situation and started issuing orders.

To an army commander, a priest, and a Wildman.

Go, Ari.

Shit.

But Finnen snorts softly, Taj grins wider, thumps his fist to his chest in a military salute, and comes to take over from Kiaran, and Kiaran...

He's still, watching me with those blue eyes. He resists Taj's efforts to pull Finn away from him for a moment, his gaze never leaving me.

Then he grabs me and hauls me against him. "You didn't stay in cave," he growls and I gasp, familiar fire running through me, at his touch, his grip, his voice, the feel of his tall body against mine. "You disobeyed."

"I couldn't stay. I had to find you—"

He smacks my ass, grabs it, presses me to what I realize is a straining erection. "I punish you later. Now I find shelter."

And he releases me and stalks off, leaving me to stare at his muscular ass, barely covered by that small loincloth, at his long legs and broad back, as he strides away.

"Your Wildman is wild," Taj comments, hauling Finnen over to me. There's a strange expression on his face.

"What?"

"Nothing. I just never thought I'd go from zero interest to getting constantly hard over a pretty, bossy omega and two annoying as hell alphas."

"You've never slept with anyone?"

"Oh, sure. Handjobs, blowjobs here and there in between campaigns. You know how the army is."

I shrug. I knew he wasn't a virgin from the things he'd said the first time we met, and yet it stings a little to know he's been with others. As if he's mine. Promised to me.

Why this sting of jealousy?

"We should get moving," Taj says. "Can you see him?"

"Yeah. Come on." I step in, press myself to Finnen's other side, and he wraps his arm around my shoulders without a word.

Which makes me worry all over again. It isn't like him to accept help without vehement protest. Just how bad is that head wound? And is he hiding any other wound under his clothes?

As the dark gathers around us, hiding the world, I still see Kiaran walking ahead of us, lights playing on his hair, like glowing moths.

How is the world changing? How are we transforming?

Most people angst over love and relationships. Few have to also bring persecution and the future of the Fae race into the equation and still...

Still, I don't think I'd have done anything differently. I can't imagine not meeting these three men, not walking with them under the moon.

Even if the path remains dark and fraught with danger.

8

ARIADNE

"Kiaran!" I can't see him anymore, the bright moth lights on his hair vanishing with him in the fall of night. "Where are you?"

"He left us," Taj grunts, "that asshole. We shouldn't have trusted him."

I understand why he's angry. Finnen is dragging between us, not a dead weight but close, and Taj's fear is palpable.

"Kiaran!" I yell. "Where the hell are you?"

"He wouldn't leave," Finnen slurs. "Mate."

"Yeah, but does he know that? In fact..." I glance at Taj. "Do *you* know that?"

"That he's our mate? My nose works just fine, thank you. He tried to kill me but I suppose it's time to kiss and make up, huh?"

I open my mouth to protest again that Kiaran hadn't been the one to attack first, but I realize I can hear the grin in his voice.

"We need to talk to him," I whisper. "See what he wants to do. He's our mate but that doesn't necessarily mean he wants to join us on this mad journey across the land looking for evasive safety. Besides, he's a man used to living alone."

"If we find him," Taj mutters.

And here I thought Finnen was the only grumpy one.

"If he left," I say and have to swallow past the sudden lump in my throat, "then he made his choice."

We're quiet after that, trudging along. I shift Finnen's arm over my shoulders, resettling it. He's heavy. His silence is unusual and worrisome. Just like Taj not volunteering to lift Finnen on his back and carry him. They are both exhausted.

Just when I'm about to suggest sitting down right here and now to rest, someone comes striding toward us, pale hair swinging over broad shoulders, pale body tall and muscular.

"Where the fuck did you go?" Taj grunts.

"I find shelter." Without missing a beat, Kiaran comes and does exactly what I'd expected Taj to do. He grabs Finnen from us, slings him over one shoulder, and turns back around. "Come. Before other jaguar find us."

———

"I didn't know we had so many jaguars," Taj says as we follow Kiaran up another hill and behind a cluster of trees. "I thought we had hunted them almost to extinction."

"Like the Fae," I mutter. "And yet here we are."

"Here we are," Taj agrees and grabs my hand when my foot slips on the trail. "Although we aren't really Fae. And that was definitely a jaguar."

"How much Fae blood do you have to have in your veins to count as Fae? It's not like we can measure it."

"What can we measure, then?"

"I would say the Council demanding our deaths is a pretty good sign that we count as Fae."

"Good point," he concedes.

But I don't feel any sense of victory at his concession. Not sure being Fae is conducive to a good life. Not something to celebrate. Not for most people.

Speaking of which...

"You don't like the Fae, Taj," I mutter as we walk behind the trees to find Kiaran settling Finnen on the ground, propping his back against a trunk. "You didn't even want to be with us when we met you. Didn't want to be one of us. Your words, not mine."

"I..." He looks away, shoves a hand through his wild dark hair. "Fuck, I know, okay? This is all fucking insane."

"You're telling me."

He grunts and I glance sideways at him. His expression is pained. "It may not seem like it, *kora*, but I want this. I want you, and I want Finnen, and I may still be unsure about this Wildman of yours, but so far, I happen to think that your taste in men is spectacular."

It startles a laugh out of me. "You're just saying that because you're one of those men."

He grins at me and it's sharp and dangerous and sexy. "Of course."

"You do realize that I may add more men to the group." I swallow hard, force myself to continue. "It's what a Fae-blooded omega does, apparently. Gather a clan around her."

"I know."

"And you don't mind?"

He turns and grabs me around the waist, pulling me to him, then his mouth is on mine, swallowing my gasp. It's quick and hard and hot and leaves me trembling when he draws back to gaze down at me with glittering gray eyes.

"I can't tell you now how I will feel about all this tomorrow," he says with ferocious frankness, "but, Ari... trust me when I say that I'm willing to give it a try, because the way I feel about you and Finnen? I can't quite put it into words without making it sound ridiculous and I can't have that when I feel like my heart is about to burst. Add to that the way I want you, the way I want to have you on every surface, in every position, in every hour of every day and I can't fight it. I can only go with the flow. If this is a Fae thing, if it's just my nature, an ancient instinct controlling me, I can't say. But I admire you and I respect Finnen, and that's not something physical. It's much more than that. Know what I mean?"

Choked up, I nod and I open my mouth to say that I think I do, even though he hasn't given me any real assurance about the future but how could he, anyway? And then...

A shift in scents and I'm already turning away, racing toward the others—

"No! Finn, don't!"

Kiaran is on his back and Finnen has him by the neck, choking him—and I have a brief moment of wondering whether the choking sensation I felt earlier was really mine, really born of emotion, or if I somehow felt one of my mates choking.

And Kiaran... he's not doing anything to defend himself. He has his hands wrapped around Finnen's wrists and he's gazing up at him but not putting any effort in stopping Finnen from ending him.

"Kiaran! No!" I fall to my knees next to them, and grab one of Finnen's corded arms, fighting to wrestle it off my Wildman. "Please, stop. You're killing him!"

Finnen's teeth are bared and he's panting. Fresh blood is dripping down the side of his face from the head wound and his cheeks are pale.

"Finn, dammit." Taj bends and grabs Finnen, pulls and pulls until he hauls him off Kiaran. They both fall down, Taj on his ass, Finnen on top of him. "What the fuck, man?"

Finnen curses, elbows him and scrambles off him. "Fuck off."

"But... what happened?" I whisper, still on my knees beside

Kiaran who is coughing and rubbing at his throat. I run a hand over his bare chest and he grabs it, presses it against his racing heart. "Are you all right, Kia?"

He coughs some more but nods, his gaze moving from my face to Finn's thunderous one. "I'm hard to kill."

"Finn." Taj is on his feet again and he has his arms folded over his chest. "What the fuck went down there? Did he try to hurt you? After he attacked me, I have to know, have to see if he's a danger to us."

Finn huffs, wipes the back of his hand over his mouth. "He tried to... to grope me," he finally spits out the words, his cheekbones crimson.

"Grope?" I stare at him in incomprehension. "Grope what?"

An interesting silence spreads.

Sitting up, Kiaran makes a muffled sound that's almost a snort.

And then Taj groans. "Oh, ho. He groped you? Groped your cock?" The army commander suddenly doubles over and produces a sound like a whine. "Holy gods."

Concerned, I jump to my feet and touch his arm. "Taj? Oh, for..."

He's *laughing*. Tears are streaming down his cheeks. He's laughing so hard he can barely breathe. "He... He... groped him..."

"What's so damn funny about that?" Finnen demands. "Just because you think you can go kissing me any time you like—"

"You kissed him again?" I turn back to Taj who is trying to catch his breath.

He wipes at his eyes. "Yeah, I did. That going to be a problem?"

"No, I..." Heat races through me at the mental image my mind helpfully provides—of the two of them in an embrace, hard mouths locked together, lust fueling them, their hard cocks—

"He *looked*," Kiaran mutters, heaving himself to his feet, brows drawn together. "At my cock. He wanted."

"I didn't— I never!" Finnen splutters, and it's my turn to start laughing. "What's so goddamn funny! Briareus's dick!"

That only makes me laugh more and I turn away, trying to compose myself, even as more heat spreads through me, making my belly cramp.

Finnen was looking at Kiaran's crotch. He was interested. Knowing Finnen, his violent denial is all the more proof of it.

And Kiaran decided to help out.

At least it looks like my boys do find each other attractive. That's good. Let's hope that once we explain the situation to Kiaran, he won't run away as fast and far as his feet can carry him.

———

"I need to go back for my horse," Taj says, frowning. "I hope the jaguars haven't eaten him."

"Tomorrow morning." I'm sandwiched between him and Finnen, grateful for their warmth, and Finnen is already out. He dozed off the moment we settled down for the night, his face drawn and pale.

Kiaran is sitting a few feet away, ostensibly keeping watch. He hasn't said so, and maybe he's just annoyed with all of us and doesn't care about lying down in one big sandwich of bodies. Is it wrong that I worry he might be cold?

I turn toward Taj, place a hand on his cheek, feeling the rough stubble underneath. "Let me check your wound."

"It's fine, *kora*. I'd tell you if I was dying. I'm not as pigheaded as Finn."

"Not sure about that," I mutter, then sigh when he lifts and presses his much bigger hand to my face. "For all it's worth, Taj, I'm sorry you got caught in this mess of a situation."

"Don't be. I'm not sorry."

"How can you not be?"

"Listen... my life in the army was many things. It was pretty good, comfortable, safe. I was tolerated. I was even admired by some. My position was coveted. My looks were envied. I could have continued like that, advanced higher in the ranks, found a permanent lover, eventually retired if I survived. But..."

"But?"

"I wasn't happy. I wasn't accepted for who I am. Nobody cared for me, not really, and I never cared about anyone else. There was an emptiness in me, a hole I couldn't fill. Not to mention that our latest orders were to hunt down and capture people like you and me, take them to either the Central or the Summer Capital to throw into jail or execute. That sooner or later they would have come for me, too. And even so..."

"Taj..."

"Even so, I would have stayed. Understand this, I've never had any other home than the army, but you... You make me feel like I'm home."

"I'm not sure," I whisper, closing my eyes as his callused fingers stroke over my temple, my neck, making me shiver. "I don't know if I'm the better choice. Home means safety. I'm probably leading you to your death."

"Or to freedom," he says, just as softly. "To a world where we don't have to hide. Finnen mentioned that in the south, in the Rising Moon Lands, things are different."

"It's a hope more than a fact, I think. His family... his parents died trying to help people like us."

"We have to ask him about it when he's awake and not freaking out over your Wildman touching him inappropriately."

I grin, and Taj grins back. "Kiaran has to learn some boundaries, and as for Finn... Do you think he can learn to relax and accept his desires?"

"We'll teach him all about sex."

I gasp a laugh. "I wish I could help, but I hardly know anything beyond the basics and that's only in theory."

"I'll teach you, too."

"Will you?" Familiar fire pools in my belly. "I feel so... frigging strange about wanting you three all the time. Like, I should be ashamed. Like, I should feel guilty for wanting it."

"You should never feel ashamed or guilty," he says fiercely. "Every woman has the right to satisfy her desires, pleasure her body, and you are a Fae-blooded omega. Your desires are stronger than the average woman's, or even the average omega's. Once you go into full heat, it will be magnificent."

"Magnificently bad, you mean," I grumble, my face burning along with my body. "I'll be a sex maniac."

"And what's more beautiful than your woman wanting you?" He dips his head, kisses me, breaking the contact too soon, leaving me gasping. "A woman giving into desire?"

A sob catches in my throat. "Taj..."

"It will be all right. We will be there."

That's reassuring, but... "Why do we have to wait for that? I want you now."

"You'll need your entire harem, *kora*, your entire clan."

"So I can't have sex until then? I'll frigging die of need."

He chuckles, a warm dark trickle of a sound. "I didn't say that. You'll need your entire clan when you go into heat. That doesn't mean you can't have sex before. It just... won't satisfy you the way you think it will."

"Why not?" My voice is a needy whine and I hate it.

But he grins again. "Because that's the way it is, kitten. Unless you can conceive, the pain in you won't go away."

"But—"

"I'm telling you, I'm going into this with my eyes wide open. I know how it all works. Trust me?"

I press myself to him. "Taj—"

Just then, Finnen turns back around and wraps himself around me with a small grunt, making me squawk in surprise, something long and hard pressing into the small of my back. "Ari," he breathes, still asleep.

Taj starts laughing quietly, rolling onto his back and throwing an arm over his eyes. "Not only is he cockblocked, he's cockblocking the rest of us. Unbelievable, that priest."

I start laughing, too. Despite the pain of need in my belly, it's strangely cute and heartwarming that Finnen is holding me like that in his sleep, exciting that he's dreaming of me and wants me even in his sleep.

Kiaran turns his head to stare at us, a dark shape in the night, outline silvered by the light of the crescent moon, his tangled pale locks a bright white. "Okay?" he asks.

It calms me down. I reach a hand out to him. "Join us, Kia. Come lie down with us."

"I can keep watch." Taj sits up, rubs his eyes. "You should get some rest, Kiaran."

Kiaran doesn't move from the spot, gazing at him.

"Did you understand what I said?" Taj gets up, unfolding his long body. "Come lie down—"

"I understand." My Wildman shakes his head. "I keep watch. You do as you like."

"You don't trust me to keep us safe, huh?" Taj ambles over to Kiaran and sits down beside him. "Fess up."

Kiaran huffs and it's frigging cute. He so obviously doesn't feel the need to reply.

I watch my two men sitting side by side, while Finnen clutches me to his chest, murmuring dream words in my ear, his breath warm on my neck. I watch as Kiaran unabashedly stares at Taj, gaze moving from his head to his chest, his crotch, his legs. Of my three men, he seems to be the least inhibited. He has no barriers, no moral boundaries hammered into him by society. He wants us and doesn't seem to care that it's obvious.

Taj returns the interested look, though he seems more bemused than anything else. Bemused and thoughtful, giving Kiaran a once-over that seems to dig beyond the surface. Appraising. Assessing. But also appreciative, I think, when he shifts on the ground and pushes a hand between his legs, probably to give his hard-on some relief.

His hard-on that I caused or a new one, caused by the handsome Wildman sitting beside him?

There's so much to find out, to explore. I just hope we get the time and that no jaguar and no army come after us in our sleep.

9

KIARAN

Taj sits down beside me. He has dark hair and pale eyes and he has a hardness about him, a toughness speaking of rough times. His mouth moves a lot, smiling, grinning, smirking. I can't tell if it's real. You smile when you're happy and relaxed.

He's not relaxed at all.

I don't think he likes me. I did cut him, then stole the girl he obviously wants. So it makes sense.

He wants me, too, though. Like with the other one, I can tell and I don't need to see his crotch to know he's hard.

But he's unsure of me. Of what I might do. Where my loyalties lie. He's protective of the other two, and I appreciate that.

I understand it.

Still don't know what my role is, my place in this group.

You don't have a place, I tell myself. *They are a... a family. Yes, that's what it's called. And it's not your family. You have no family anymore.*

Haven't had one in so long you hardly remember what it feels like.

I don't know why I'm still here.

"So your name is Kiaran," Taj says, still gazing at me with those intense pale eyes. "What's your family name?"

I shrug. "I don't remember."

"You're a Drakoryas. A berserker. Living alone in the wilderness, sworn to fight in the Emperor's army if the occasion arises."

"If there is war," I mutter. "They said that."

"The recruiters. Always looking for more Wildmen to add to the ranks, always fearing another great war that will require every resource available to man, even though the Fae are vanquished and gone."

He keeps stating facts. What is he after? I gaze at him, trying to read his signs like I read the signs of the forest and the hills, of the animals and the elements.

"How old were you when they found you and recruited you to the cause?" he asks. "When they told you that you were a berserker, a soldier of his Serenity the Emperor and would be called by means of a fire at the top of a hill nearby if you were needed? Or did they just mark your cave and said they'd be back if you were needed, no promises and no threats?" He stops. "Do you understand what I'm saying?"

"Yes," I say, annoyed.

More or less. Thinking is fine, half-images, half-words. Speaking, though... I'm out of practice, and he uses many words I don't know.

Out of practice of speaking and being around people.

It's easier with her. There's a sweetness about her, a softness that calms me down, that hooks me and gently pulls me to her.

This man sitting beside me is the opposite of her. He's more like me, all hard edges, planes and angles.

"So how old were you?"

I lift my hand, then the other, frowning down at them,

trying to count. I knew how to count when I found myself in these hills. "Seven."

"Seven?" He frowns back at me. "You were a child."

Sure I was. So what? All of us were children once. So I wait for him to explain or ask. I don't know what he wants from me.

"You've lived here alone all this time? How many years now... eleven? twelve?"

I throw up my hands. He's asking too much. After all this time, how am I expected to count and talk and do all the things humans do, when I grew up like an animal in the woods?

A fist closes around my chest and I can't breathe. With a grunt, I scramble to my feet and pace a few steps away.

I'd have left already, only... Only *she* is here, and her perfume is like a rope around my neck, around my chest, around my dick, around every part of me, and I can't deny that it's not just that. Not just her perfume. And not just her. I want... things. These people make me want things, with them, that I can't name and can't understand.

"Wait. Where are you going?" Taj comes after me and I stumble further away, to keep some distance. I don't know how to deal with him.

I understand protecting people. I understand pleasure and pain. But I don't understand this need to be with them. I've met other Wildmen over the years but the only thing they made me want was to stay away from them.

"Kiaran," she calls out from where she lies in Finnen's arms, and I step further back, staggering and almost falling down the slope. "No!"

I lift my hands, as much in reassurance as to keep them away.

Finnen can't see. I realized when I first met him. He seems to be looking at me now, though, sitting up on the ground and getting on his feet.

"Now what?" he says. "Stop scaring our mate away, Taj."

"Says the man who tried to strangle him," Taj mutters. "Hey, Kiaran. It's fine. I'll stop asking questions if you don't feel like answering. Don't go anywhere just yet, okay?"

Mate?

The word echoes in my ears, like something from a dream.

It means something to me. I dig through my memories, struggling to remember, and my head aches.

"Kiaran, careful! Don't move!" Taj is edging toward me, a hand held out to me, and I can't decide if it's a mirror of my gesture—to keep me away, to keep me calm—or if he's trying to catch me. "Don't take another step."

Slowly his words filter in, too slowly—it takes a long while for my mind to register the meanings, though it's getting better.

Not fast enough, though, it seems.

I take a step back.

Taj yells out my name.

Ariadne screams.

Finnen curses, grabbing onto Ariadne who's starting toward me, both hands reaching for me.

I fall.

There's solid earth and then there's nothing as I tumble down the slope, the sky with its yellow moon turning to stone and pain, and then nothing.

———

"Kiaran! Holy Goddess, he can't hear me. Kiaran!"

I reach out blindly a hand to stop her from talking. "Ariadne," I whisper.

"Looks like he can hear you just fine," a male voice says. I think it's Finnen's. "Lucky you didn't fall far, Wildman."

My head is ringing but I manage to open my eyes. She's bent over me, her hair a curtain around her face, the half-moon crowning her as if she's an empress meant for a throne.

"My parents were mates," I whisper.

"What?"

"I know that word. *Mates.*"

She puts her hands on my face, over my cheeks, and smiles down at me. She looks like a goddess of the earth, her eyes so big they could swallow me whole. "Good. You are our mate, Kiaran. You have a bond with us. You must have smelled it. Smelled how we fit together."

Is that what it means? Wonder fills me. Or maybe it's relief at making sense of the strange feelings. A need. A bond.

"You're an alpha," she says. "As are they. And I'm an omega. We have Fae blood in us, as do you. Fate is pushing us together, but..." Her small mouth twists a little. "But that doesn't mean you have to do anything. If you don't want to be in our clan, if you would rather stay here, in your cave, your solitude, we will understand."

"You have a clan?"

"We *are* a clan. A family."

Family.

My earlier thoughts return, fluttering wings like sparrows in the snow, about how I barely remember the word, the feeling, but with them, with her, it becomes familiar again.

It's all too much, and the wonder and relief turn into panic, the pounding in my head rising to a deafening buzz.

Dragging myself onto my side, I retch, my stomach turning itself inside out, sourness scouring my throat.

"Oh no. He must have hit his head." Ariadne sounds dismayed. "Like you did, Finn."

"I didn't retch," he says, annoyed. He often sounds annoyed. Something must be bothering him. I get like that when fireants burn me and the area itches for days.

"Or maybe we pushed him too much," Tash says thoughtfully. "Me with my questions, you with the information and the options he's never had before."

I blink. Of all of them, I hadn't expected him to be the one to get this.

"You don't have to do anything, Kia," she says gently.

"Do you understand, Wildman?" Finnen mutters. "Take your time to decide. If you prefer the wilderness and your privacy, that's up to you."

Looks like I'm expected to say something anyway. Like it's my turn to give some information.

"I... was alone... for long time." I rub my mouth. My throat burns. "I'm not... an idiot."

"No, that would be Taj," Finnen says and I think I hear a smirk in his voice. "Definitely."

Is he serious? Is he teasing?

I'm not sure I understand this man. Finnen. He's strong, obviously stubborn, but also denies what he feels, what his body demands. How can you trust someone who is lying to himself all the time?

How can I trust any of them? I've spent my life in distrust. It saved me again and again, from avoiding brightly colored mushrooms to approaching other people. She broke that cycle, but what if I've made a mistake?

Straightening, shifting onto my knees, I wipe at my mouth. "I don't know you. Any of you."

"Fair point," Ariadne says. "I am Ariadne Vespere. I was an acolyte of holy Artume until recently, at the fort of Artare."

"And I was a commander in the Imperial army," Taj says. "Up until a couple of days ago."

I frown. Turn to look at Finnen. "And you?"

"I am a priest," he says stiffly.

Something's odd about the way he speaks his line, as opposed to the others, and it takes me a long moment to sort it out.

I *am* a priest.

Not I *was*.

I don't know what that means—for me, for them, for everything. And it doesn't help me decide if I should follow them—for a clan, for a family—or turn my back on them and trudge back to my cave, my familiar world and my way of living.

Until I am called to fight in the army.

Or die of loneliness. I've been lonely for so long it's a festering wound in my chest.

But I also like being alone. I'm used to it. It's easier to think when I don't have three other persons talking, asking questions, invading my space, needing my attention.

I thought the choice was clear-cut. I'm lonely. But I'm used to hunting, fighting big animals, gathering fruit and nuts, preparing furs to wear. It all takes time and concentration, and gives a result. Being around people is... messy. Unpredictable. Tricky.

And this mate business... what does it mean long term? Why are they here? Where are they going? What do they really want? That's the burning question. Her touch mesmerizes me, her perfume arouses me, I like being near her, I want to keep her safe... I want to sniff at the two men, touch them, see if they are nice, if they are as interesting as they seem...

But Finnen tried to choke me for trying to touch and Taj is suspicious of me, and Ariadne... what am I to do with her?

"I'll stay with you." I sit up and lift a hand when Ariadne smiles and starts talking. "For a while. To get to know you. To understand."

Her smile falls and she valiantly fights to get it back. "Good. That's great. It's..."

"It's something," Taj says. "It's a chance."

"A chance," I whisper.

"I also want to get to know you." Taj reaches down, and after a moment I realize he's giving me a hand up. "I mean, I don't think you're a bad person. You did save our lives out there, when you killed that jaguar. But why were you in that shelter the other day? Why did you attack me?"

"I followed... her scent." I decide to accept his help, and I let him haul me to my feet. "I never smelled anything... so good... in my life."

"I feel that, my man. I know what you mean."

She steps closer, takes my other hand. "For what it's worth, you smell good, too, Kia."

"Like an animal," I mutter.

A soft snicker escapes her. "Like a man. Like an alpha."

"If he's staying with us," Finnen says, coming to place a hand on my arm, "he has to be taught some manners."

"Manners?" Their touch is disconcerting, disorienting... disarming.

"I think Finnen means... no groping without permission," Ariadne says. "That's a good general rule out there, you know."

"But you have to learn to read the other person," Taj says. "See if they say no but mean yes."

"Permission," I breathe. "So I have to ask every time he wants my touch? Even if I can see he does?"

"You..." Finnen growls softly.

"We can work it out together," Taj interrupts him. "Now come get some rest." He grabs my forearm and I let him drag me back up the slope I rolled down on. "Believe it or not, this is a lot to take for all of us."

10

ARIADNE

Kiaran is coming with us.

This turn of events makes me want to smile. Even if he keeps apart when we lie down again to sleep, and keeps a few feet apart when we walk, usually stalking ahead of us, it's such a relief.

I have three of my mates with me, and although I wish we were locked up in a nice, warm house to get to know each other better, in every sense of the word, I can't deny that something inside of me has relaxed.

It's not enough, though. The ache in my belly has returned, and with it flashes of alternating heat and cold that have me sweating one moment and shivering the next. The men insisted I ride on Taj's horse—found uneaten and unharmed, thankfully—and I can't deny it's a huge relief. As we wend our way through the plain, keeping close to the hills and away from the main road leading to the Summer Capital and the south, exhaustion drags on all of us. We haven't had food in days, though at least we got water from streams running through the plain, and the cold is closing in on us.

Kiaran went and brought furs from his cave before we left

his area of the hills, as well as jerky. Fortified thus, wearing mismatched furry shawls, we wend our way into Winter and the unknown.

We'll need food before we drop and end our journey right here, among the rocky outcrops and thorny bushes with nothing to show for our big decisions and repeated, daring escapes from the claws of death.

When Kiaran hurries back to us a few mornings later, even lifting my head is an effort. He's wearing a short mantle made from a jaguar skin, a sort of short leather skirt and short boots, and has pulled his pale shoulder-length locks into a low tail.

But it's his expression that alerts me something's up.

"What is it, Kia?" I look down at him as he falls into step beside the horse and places a hand on my calf. He likes doing that, coming close and touching me, as if that gives him comfort. I know it does, for me. "What did you see?"

"Houses," he says, his voice soft with some unnamed emotion. "Houses together."

"A village?" I glance at Finnen and Taj who have slowed down and are watching us. "A village lies ahead?"

"Big," Kiaran says. "Town?"

"A town! We could get food, provisions," Taj says. "Maybe there's an inn to stay the night. No more sleeping under the stars. We could sleep on actual beds!"

"With what coin?" Finnen glowers at nothing in particular. "Or are we to steal?"

"Goes against your priestly code, does it, now?" Taj mutters.

"Damn right it does. And it should go against an army commander's moral code, too."

"The army isn't a sheltered little world like the Temple, priest. Steal? You bet. We loot and pillage."

"You also murder and rape, but I..."

"What?"

Finnen shrugs. "Never mind."

"Spit it out, priest."

"I don't think you'd do that sort of thing," Finnen finally says.

With Taj momentarily rendered speechless, I tell Kiaran, "Take us to this town. We need this."

His blue eyes meet mine and heat flares in them, matched by the heat washing over my body.

Without another word, he takes the reins and pulls the horse toward the west. We are moving away from the hills and following, at a distance, a small river, a tributary of the great river Ekelon, the river that passes through the capital of the Empire and down through the Summer Capital, too.

The plan is to turn away from its course soon so as to avoid getting too close to the dreaded city, the summer seat of the Emperor and southern headquarters of the Temple. The place of our planned execution.

Taking the trade routes leading south, through the plan and the salt marshes, closing in to the borders of the Empire with the great port kingdoms of the Rising Moon Lands, particularly Tethia that is the closest.

If Finnen is right... If there is sanctuary for us... If their King really is pro-Fae and continues being so... Everything hinges on that and yet we can't know for sure until we reach the southern territories and the independent Rising Moon Lands.

And if won't count for anything unless we find food and rest, recover enough to make that journey.

"I bet you have coin," Finnen is saying to Taj. "You do, don't you? Hidden somewhere about your person, like those knives in your boots?"

"Wouldn't you like to know." Taj chuckles. "And what if I do? What do you wanna bet?"

"You know I have nothing to bet with."

"So you seem to think. If I have coin, what will you give me?"

"There you go again with silly games—"

"A kiss."

Finn stiffens. "Like I said. You like to tease."

"I wasn't teasing."

My mouth quirks. I like it. I shouldn't like it so much, perhaps, that they desire each other. I should want all their attention on me, all their lust for me only, but it wouldn't work out well in the end, would it? They'd probably be jealous of each other, fight with each other, be dissatisfied and annoyed, especially if I add more men to the clan.

And look at you, Ari, thinking about expanding your clan, collecting more men like it's something women do the world over.

But I will have to, won't I? Expand it. Until it reaches the right amount, the right men, the right combination of scents and voice cadences and attributes to satisfy my inner omega, satisfy it that I have everything I need to create a good family. A safe, warm, perfect place, surrounded by my mates.

I shiver.

I haven't read all the books Finnen and Taj seem to have studied about the Fae and their biology and culture, but all this seems to be instinctive. Like I know it in the marrow of my bones, like it makes sense in some mysterious, unknowable way.

Sidde Drakai.

"If I allow another kiss," Finnen grumbles, "you'd better have enough coin to buy us a good dinner with beer and a clean room with enough beds for all of us."

"Woo. You drive a hard bargain." Taj is grinning and sauntering down the trail through the fields like he's on his way to a picnic. "The bet is on."

I catch Kiaran frowning back at them and oh gods, he has to have doubts, hearing all that banter. A man who's been alone for—how long? Most of his life, it seems, and yet he's coming with us. Giving it a try.

Meanwhile, Finnen and Taj are acting like young acolytes fighting over a piece of bread at dinner, and yet it's all about attraction, as I realize more and more. Attraction and the dynamics of this unconventional relationship, both men vying for the top and testing the limits of their fascination, their pull toward each other, the limits of their distinct personalities. They like each other and have been looking after each other. But they still aren't sure about their exact place in this clan.

Does Kiaran see that? He said it himself, he's not an idiot—but when it comes to human relationships he might as well be. Relationships, boundaries, nuances.

He's as innocent of them as I am of sexual pleasure.

And let's not even touch the topic of Finnen and his general flat-out refusal to consider said pleasure. Or Taj's divided loyalties, no matter his reassurances.

Yes, one can have doubts. I harbor some, so why shouldn't Kiaran? But I want to convince him to stay with us, if nothing else because, now he's with us, I can't imagine not having him around.

The cold breeze blows his scent over to me and I blink back tears. I want him. I want them. Taj said it won't satisfy me the way I think it will—having sex with them now—but it's wearing me down. Who knows how long it will take to find my other mates, to complete the circle? The way I feel right now, my heat can't be far away.

And if I go into heat without my full clan... What happens then?

Fear grips me, and I want to ask Taj or Finnen, but I don't dare. I'm not sure I want to know the answer. Many human women die in childbirth, but I remember reading that many Fae omegas died in heat because they didn't have a full harem.

But how? How did they die? *Goddess...*

By now we are all stumbling with exhaustion, so when Taj calls out, "There's the town!" a weight lifts off me.

It's a fortified one, sitting on a low rise in the land, a grey construction resembling the rocky hills where Kiaran lived and where we took shelter with the army.

And on top of the walls fly the banners of the Temple.

———

"There's a branch of the Temple here," I say, in case everyone else missed it. Finnen for sure hasn't seen the banners, so there's that. "We should leave."

"And go where?" Taj says. "It's getting dark."

"Like every night," Finnen mutters. "Your point being?"

Kiaran has stopped, his hand on the horse's bridle, his blue eyes unreadable as he gazes at the town ahead.

"Stop being a smartass, Finn," Taj says, "and consider our options. We need food. Unless we want to hunt and eat raw meat, or grass from the plain, which I have done and don't necessarily recommend, this is where we need to be. We need provisions, we need a good night's sleep, and we need information, otherwise we'll be blundering direction south and courting death."

"Courting death is an everyday expectancy."

Taj sighs. "May the Gods help me not to kill this man."

"Maybe you need to pray to other gods. Army gods like killing. Not that you'd ever stand a chance of killing me." Finnen frowns. "I should probably train you..."

"Finn!"

Finnen bows his head, a smirk tugging at his lips. "Yes?"

"Give it a rest, you two." I sigh. "What do you think, Finn? Should we enter this town? How probable is it they'll recognize us? Well, you in particular. Have you ever passed through here?"

"I wish I could say it doesn't look familiar," Finnen says drily, "but alas, I can't see it."

"Which town is this?" I turn to Taj. "Any ideas?"

"If I remember the map correctly and if I'm not hopelessly lost, it might be Martus or Satria," Taj says. "One of the small stops on the trading route toward the south and of course the Summer Capital."

"No. Doesn't ring any bells," Finnen says.

"I vote we go in," Taj says. "Kiaran? What do you think?"

The Wildman doesn't speak, still gazing at the town.

"Kia?" I lean over the horse's side, but he's too far to touch. "Are you okay?"

He harrumphs.

No choice but to take that as a yes. I seem to be the only one with misgivings about this decision, but the thought of a warm meal and a soft bed is way too tempting to resist.

The horse's hooves clop on the paved street leading up the low hill, Taj taking up the front, Finnen by his side. We are at the rear, Kiaran and me, following them past low stone-built houses with small gardens and smoking ovens in their yards.

A town on the road leading to the Summer Capital, Eremis, the traditional summer residence of the Emperor.

A big city with gleaming temples to the gods and singing fountains in the squares, statues hewn from marble and blue stone quarried from the mountains of Athus which are looming in the distance and laced with gold bought from the south.

The old Fae capital, according to some tales.

I've read about it. I've even seen some pictures. I've wanted to see it with my own eyes, experience a city that purportedly never sleeps, full of beautiful things and elegant people. But it will never happen. It's a gleaming place of death we have to avoid at all costs.

This small town built out of the grey rock dotting the landscape with its twin turrets over the open gate and the neat two-story houses lining the street will have to do...

11

ARIADNE

Finding the inn proves easy. Not far from the main street of the town, there is a big wooden sign hanging on a façade with an arrow pointing down a side alley. 'The Dragon Fang Inn.'

Ominous. But as the men turn into the alley, Kiaran pulling the horse, we find a simple albeit tall gate that's wide open, and laughter and aromas of roasted meat waft over to us, making my stomach growl like an actual dragon of old.

We cross a square yard to reach the two-story building, the second floor studded with doors to its many rooms. The plain entrance was quite deceptive. It's a big place with a gurgling fountain at its center, stables for the horses on one side and fruit trees on the other.

Kiaran leads me toward the stables and a harassed-looking stable hand appears to snatch the reins from him. He growls when the stable hand starts pulling the horse toward the stables with me still on it and I'm at a great vantage point to see the stable hand finally stop and actually look at him.

"Drakoryas," he whispers and scurries away.

"How would he know?" I whisper.

"It's the craziness in the eyes," Finn says, deadpan. "Hard to hide."

Kiaran reaches for me. "Come."

Without hesitation, I swing my leg over the saddle and slip down the horse's flank, trusting him to catch me.

His strong arms come around me, hauling me against his hard body, not allowing my feet to touch the ground. Instinctively I hook my knees around his hips and his hands go under my ass, keeping me in place.

Not the most dignified position for a woman to be publicly seen in, perhaps, but by the time I think to try and regain my feet, I'm lost in his gaze. His eyes are so blue, like a sea, and I drown in them.

I haven't been in his arms, or even this close to him, since our brief time in his cave, and my breath wooshes out of me in a rush.

Then his scent seeps in, pepper and nutmeg, pine and resin, and fire rolls through me. A gasp escapes me at the sensation, the pain/pleasure of it, the sharp need for him.

He grunts, eyes widening, his grip on my ass tightening. He lowers me a little and we both gasp when I'm pressed firmly against the hard bulge of his crotch.

He's tall enough that, in this position, I'm too low to reach his mouth, kiss him, and I moan in frustration—at not being able to kiss him or touch him skin to skin, too many layers of fabric and fur between us, not a good position for him to take me and fill me up—

"Drakoryas!" someone hisses and it doesn't even make it through to my lust-addled mind. "Wildmen!"

People have gathered in the yard, observing us, the men dressed in long cloaks, and the women in long sweeping dresses, shawls hiding their hair, scrubbed clean and tidy and proper, and I wonder how I look to them.

"Drakoryas." I can hear their whispers winging like birds,

wings batting against my mind. "Wildmen. Berserkers. Madmen. Dangerous."

"Fuck. They think all of us are Wildmen." Taj starts undressing. "Take off the furs."

That manages to draw my attention away from Kiaran, and I crane my neck to watch Taj undress. My mouth goes dry as I watch my mate pull the fur mantle off him and let it drop at his feet. Underneath, his black shirt stretches beautifully over his muscular chest and arms.

"Peace!" he calls out. "We're traders, not Wildmen. Here. I have coin." He lifts both hands, silver *eremins* glinting between his fingers. "See?"

Cursing, Finnen starts pulling off the fur cape Kiaran gave him, something about gods and goats and fucking, and I wonder if he's just committed a transgression against his gods and what he'll do if he realizes later, punish himself or find some other form of self-harm to perform.

Then he turns to me. "Ari! Come on. Off with the furs."

I let him pull me off Kiaran and set me down on my feet, a little dazed, lifting my arms obediently when he mutters and tugs on the fur poncho I've been wearing over my clothes. Cold rushes over my body when he lifts the poncho off me and lets it drop to the ground, too.

"We stink," Taj says between his teeth while grinning at the gathered people. "That's not helping our cause. We need a bath. And new clothes."

"Just how much coin are you carrying with you?" Finnen mutters, and frowns. "Kiaran! Where is he?" He beckons in the general direction of our Wildman. "Furs off. Are you doing it? Ari, is he doing it?"

No. He isn't. Kiaran is standing there, frozen, eyes glassy and face drained of color, still in his furs and leather skirt and low boots. Despite the trim I gave his beard and his hair, he still looks the quintessential barbaric, bloodthirsty, mad Wildman.

Goddess, he's gorgeous. And sexy. And I can still smell him, feel his hard body against mine. I—

"For fuck's sake," Finnen growls and steps toward Kiaran.

Kiaran who growls and lifts his fists, turning a murderous glare on my priest. Teeth bared, canines looking a little too long, a little too sharp, lights flashing over his face and hands, and... smoke coming out of his nostrils?

The small crowd gasps and shuffles backward.

No, no, this can't happen. I won't let it. The blankness in Kiaran's eyes, the flat fury, that's not him, that's something else. It's as if he's lost touch with the here and now.

"Kia, no!" I step in front of him, blocking his view of Finnen, and reach out a hand to him. "Here, come here, to me."

"He's not a pet," Finnen mutters.

"Shut up, Finn."

"He's damaged."

"Which one of us isn't?"

"Ari—"

"Imagine growing up all alone in the wilderness," I grind out. "Imagine having to fend for yourself against the wild animals, the other Wildmen, the cold of winter and heat of summer, of learning to find food and clothing, shelter and fire. And imagine being alone. So very alone and afraid, having to find your own strength and get used to the echo of your own voice, your own breaths, everyone else too afraid to even approach you."

Finnen' inhale is sharp. "I can... I can imagine that."

I nod, turn my attention back to Kiaran. I reach for one of his big fists and at my touch, he blinks. And blinks again. "It's okay," I say. "You're with us. Let's take off your furs, yeah?"

He doesn't reply, doesn't say a word, but his eyes drop to my hand on his hand and he doesn't move a muscle as I reach for the leather knot keeping his fur mantle in place. Slowly I undo the knot, finding his sharp blue gaze on me every time I lift my eyes, then push the mantle off his broad shoulders.

The fire in those blue depths is magnetic.

"All we want is a room for the night and dinner," Taj says loudly, breaking the spell. He's still waving the coins around. He looks like he's fending off a pack of wolves with the silver. "We've traveled far and need provisions. We won't stay long in your town. Are we good?"

Finally, a heavily-set woman steps forward, a suspicious look on her face. "Give them here." She takes the coins from Taj's hands—all the coins—and hefts them in her hand, a thoughtful line creasing her brow. "The *eremins* look real."

"Of course they are real," Taj says, his grin fraying around the edges.

"Hm." She shoves the coins into a leather purse hanging from her belt. She's dressed in a cotton dress, but it's the expensive kind, the hem embroidered with blue flowers, her cloak trimmed with silk, her wooden headdress glinting with copper or silver inlays.

"Are we good?" Taj asks again, stepping in front of the rest of us, hands held out to the sides. "That coin should cover everything we are asking for."

"It's enough for a room and dinner, and for your horses to have some hay," she says with a toss of her head toward the inn. "If you want anything more, you'll need to pay up."

"Fuck," Taj breathes but he turns to us and nods. "Come on. Let's at least get our money's worth. We've earned it."

———

Whether we've earned it or not, the inn-keeper doesn't seem to care either way. She obviously doesn't like us, doesn't like a group that looks like berserkers, or like beggars at best, staying within her walls and scaring off her well-paying customers.

She leads us up a steep, rickety wooden staircase to the upper floor, and I exchange a look with Taj. He shrugs. Normally upper floor rooms are reserved for the richer customers, as the air flows better and less vermin reaches it.

Of course, soon enough I see her goal. It's a small chamber, wedged between the staircase and the rest of the rooms. Not a storage room, at least not anymore, and the two narrow beds shoved against two walls can't possibly fit the four of us, even if she assumes (and rightly so) that I wouldn't mind sleeping in the same bed any or all of my men.

Not something any decent girl would be expected to do.

I open my mouth to protest, and she lifts a finger forbiddingly.

"This is it, take it or leave it. And stay away from my other customers," she all but growls, in a fairly good imitation of Finnen. "Don't come down unless it's to leave. Do you understand me?"

"But, dinner," I start.

"Dinner will be brought up to you."

"We need clothes," Taj says.

"Do I look like a seamstress?"

"Then send us one."

She gives him a once over and relaxes a little, probably deciding he's the least wild-looking of our bunch. "I can sell you some second-hand clothes I have lying around, if you have the coin."

"We have to see their state first," Taj says carefully, "and if they fit us."

She steps closer to him, sniffs and wrinkles her nose. "You should save your coin for a bath."

"If possible, we'll have that, too." Taj returns her stony glare with an easy smile. "If your ladyship could see to it."

"Hm." Her gaze moves from his face down to his chest, and

lower. "What are you doing with this bunch of losers, a fine man like you? You're obviously not a Wildman."

"You don't seem to have any respect for the Drakoryas." Taj's voice goes flat, his smile fading. "Dragonkin. The secret of the Empire. They're the fiercest warriors in the Imperial army, the terror of our enemies, men who have nothing to gain from throwing themselves into battle except their loyalty to the empire. They often give up their lives for us, often used to save the lives of regular troops, with no compensation should they survive and no benefit apart from a small piece of land, perhaps, and a hut to live in. Men who spend their lives alone and living as beasts, forgotten by us all. But you think you can talk dirt about them? Use their name as an insult?"

"Whoa." I'm staring at Taj, a flower of warmth blooming in my chest. I didn't know he felt that way about Wildmen. I thought he considered them mindless beasts but hearing him defending them is... beautiful.

Kiaran produces a small sound and I turn toward him. His eyes are shining too bright and I don't know what's going through his head but I step up to him and take his hand.

"Apologies, my lord," the inn-keeper says, subdued. "I didn't know you were an army man."

"I'm not." Taj shakes his head and turns away. "Not anymore."

"Once a soldier, always a soldier. I'll send up your dinner and some clothing for you to take a look at, my lord. I have... my son is in the army. He's..." Again she stops, uncertainty in every line of her face. "I'll have more blankets sent up, too."

And with a hurried curtsy, she walks out, leaving us for the first time alone, all four of us within four walls. Hopefully, the inn-keeper will keep her promise of food because I'm famished. Only thing left, I think, is to hope the men won't kill each other tonight.

Fingers crossed staying here was a good idea after all...

12

TAJ

I wish I could say that outing my profession was a planned gamble. But it was only weariness and annoyance that made me give a whole damn speech about the Drakoryas to the bitch running this fine establishment, and I honest to the gods hope that I haven't made a huge mistake.

If rumors of a military man with a bunch of Wildmen—and a wild woman, probably—reach the ears of the Temple or the army, we're toast. I have no doubt that everyone is currently looking for us. If we're lucky, they think we're dead in a ditch somewhere and have turned their attention to other matters.

Depends how afraid they are of a Fae omega and her clan.

The existing clues point to a healthy dose of fear.

As in, a fucking ton of it. The Temple is either terrified or horrified at the perspective, and why not both? After all, the imperial council issued that damn missive about Fae-blood and the land is up in arms about it. Most people don't need much of an incentive to start rounding others up and torching them. There's a kind of magic in hurting others. You think it will help you. That their pain will turn your luck around.

It never works, though. You never get what you want.

Then again, it's never stopped people over the centuries from giving it a go, you know... just in case it was them causing your bad luck, your bad crops, your sick animals, your cheating spouse. Not your fault, but theirs.

We're a sad lot, we humans. Not that I think the Fae were any better. We obviously share some distant ancestor somewhere down the line, or we wouldn't have been able to mix in the first place. So it makes sense that we share more, more than families and babies, all the good and bad traits.

"Taj, come on," Ariadne says.

She has placed our fur mantles over the two beds for extra warmth. A vent in the wall brings heat from the central fireplace into the room, though, so that it's cozy. I'm in danger of thawing, of relaxing, and it's what I wanted but now I'm fucking scared that the reality of this whole crazy endeavor will take advantage and shove past the shock, becoming crystal clear.

I have left my old life behind. It's over. Too late to go back.

And though I've accepted it, or think I have, it's still a blow.

I wonder how long it will take until I've digested the truth of it and stop being shocked every time I look back.

Sorcha, Denik, Fain, the closest I've ever had to friends, lieutenants and soldiers. Not real friends but the closest to a family I've had.

I won't be seeing them again.

And despite feeling as sure as I can be that this is where I wanna be, with Ariadne and these guys, yeah, it's still a fucking punch to the guts.

"Taj." Her small hand slips into mine, warm and soft. "Are you all right?"

Turning without a word, I gather her into my arms, bury my face in her hair. Even filthy from the journey, it smells sweet, like her, and it calms me down.

She gasps softly, her arms going around my neck, and I

become damn aware of her breasts pressed to my stomach, her soft curves, the heat of her skin, the darkness in her eyes.

Calm is overrated anyway. With a returning hunger that exhaustion had dimmed, I crush our bodies and our mouths together and groan into the kiss. Oh, fuck yeah, this is what I need; she is what I want. My body and mind are in agreement, though my body has the reins right now. Dimly I remember telling her she won't be fully satisfied until she has her full clan, but what the hell do the books know? She's aroused and wet, I can smell it lacing her natural sweetness with the heavier aromas of burnt sugar, peaches and cream.

Nowhere in the books was it said that an omega had to wait for her full heat or harem to fuck, right? Nowhere does it say that it's all about babies, though those old crusty scholars who wrote them probably thought only of that.

This is about pleasuring my woman and finding my own release, it's about marking her as mine and giving myself over to her. It's about a bond that is building and building, like a house, like a nest where we will live out our days.

She rubs herself against me, and I lose the last vestiges of my control. I grab her, shove her against the closed door, lift one of her legs to wrap it around my thigh, my hard cock pressing into her belly. Layer upon layer of fabric thwarts my efforts to slide into her, not for lack of trying. I'm growling, my hands on her shirt, and the laces are already tearing, when someone grabs me from behind and hauls me back.

"What? What the fuck?" I whirl about, kicking and punching, snarling and biting, needing to claim what is mine, and find Finnen in my face, snarling right back.

"What the hell, man?" he yells in my ear. "Are you going to ravish her right here and now, with the inn-keeper due back in any moment? Want us to get kicked out in the cold of night? Where's your famous military discipline?"

Panting, I turn my glare from him to Ariadne and my heart

stops. She looks debauched, with a shredded shirt wrapped around her breasts, barely covering them, her hair loose, her lips bee-stung, her eyes kind of wide and wild.

She looks beautiful. She looks like an animal had a go at her.

Fuck.

"You're going into a rut," Finnen says.

"Aren't we all?" I mutter. "Well, except for you, of course, unflappable Reverend Brother Finn."

"Fuck you."

"I may, some other day, if you ask nicely."

"What the fuck," Finn hisses, "is wrong with you? That woman—"

The door clicks and opens, throwing Ariadne forward. Turning, I catch her in my arms and the fire returns, darkening my thoughts. Through the haze of lust, over my mate's head, I see that woman—as Finnen said—entering the room, carrying a lit oil lamp, her eyes narrowing at me.

"Your bath is being brought up," she says, putting the lamp down on the floor and frowning at us disapprovingly, "and dinner is here." She claps her hands, and two servant boys enter the room, carrying big trays laden with steaming bowls of stew, chunks of brown bread and cups of ale. "Put them on a bed, boys. You, girl, come on in."

A slight girl enters then, half-hidden behind a load of clothing, and totters to the center of the room. "Where, mistress?"

"Good gods, on the bed that has no trays on it, girl! Use your head."

The girl obediently drops the load on the other bed and steps back, eyes big and frightened in a small mousey face.

I slide my arms more firmly around Ariadne. Her face is buried against my chest, her tumble of dark wild hair all I see of her, but I feel her body against mine, every point of contact burning through me.

Dammit, I want everyone out so I can fuck my mate. Is that too much to ask? Anger rolls through me. I want to shove everyone out of my way and then rip her clothes to have her naked underneath me, put my mouth and hands everywhere before I sink into her.

"I'm being overly kind to you all," the inn-keeper is saying, her glower moving from one of us to the next. "If I hear any improper noises or find you wandering outside this room, you'll get the boot, do you hear me?"

"Yes, madam," Finnen says, ever the proper gentleman.

Kiaran only growls softly.

"Good." She claps her hands again and her toy soldiers march out, leaving the trays and clothes on the beds. "The tub is coming up. Don't spill water everywhere and make a mess." She tsks, glances at me again. "You're lucky you remind me of my son."

"Yeah," Finnen says, head cocked to the side, blind eyes thoughtful, "you are lucky, aren't you, soldier? Why don't you thank the nice lady? Thank the lady, Taj!"

It's a slap to my face, to my chest—a command, an order, and my body twangs like a chord. "Thank you," I say. "I..."

"Yes, good, fine." The inn-keeper turns around in a whirl of shawls and skirts and heads out the door. "My fault for letting a bunch of wild people into my inn, military or not. Just don't break anything or you'll pay good coin for it, got me?"

I watch her go, cold and hot warring in my body, my mind here but also back in the barracks on the plain, waiting for a command to set order to my life, to make me feel good. To make me feel I'm doing the right thing.

A pleasurable tingle is running up and down my spine, and if I wasn't hard already, I'd probably get hard now, just from this.

What the fuck, right?

What the fuck is wrong with me?

———

The tub arrives, carried into our room by two red-faced, wheezing men. It's made of wood and it's much bigger than I expected. In the army, we made do with dips in freezing rivers and streams and the occasional shower with a holed bucket set up on something high like a tree branch. I'd only heard of bath tubs, though I have a vague, washed-out memory of one at home as a child. If I didn't dream that.

Hard to tell sometimes what is a real memory and what a fancy of the mind.

Two women follow with buckets filled with hot water, which they empty inside, and they go and come back another six or seven times until the tub is half full.

The air is filling up fast with warm steam and the smell of the hard green soap the women leave on a stool by the side, along with a bath sheet.

"Oh." Even Ariadne is distracted by all this ceremony, and she pulls away from me to stare at the tub. "Wow. That inn-keeper really likes you."

I'm still standing stock still, thinking about my reaction to Finnen's command.

It was a gut reaction, I think, just a remnant from the army. I grew up in the ranks, it was my whole life. It makes sense.

But that doesn't explain the physical pleasure I felt. The arousal.

As if reading my thoughts, Finnen says, "You have a hard-on for orders?"

"Whatever," I mutter, shaken.

"How do you feel about whips and paddles?" He approaches the tub slowly, hands held out, shuffling his feet on the floor and I stare at him. I often forget he really is blind. He's just so otherworldly confident and strong that it's only in moments like this I remember it, and my chest gets a little tight at the reminder.

"Shut up," I say.

"If I command you in the right voice, will you roll over and let me rub your tummy?"

"Maybe it's something else you wanna rub," I say and grin when his head jerks toward me. "Huh, priest?"

"Let's bathe before the water gets cold. We should undress."

I turn to look at Ariadne. "Well, finally," I say, to cover up the unease still stirring in me.

Her face reddens. "I..."

"Are we all getting inside?" Kiaran has approached the tub and is sniffing at it suspiciously. "We don't fit."

Ariadne's face is turning crimson. "All of us? No, each at a t—"

"Yeah," I say, all of us. "Before the water turns cold. Right, Finn?"

"Have you lost your mind?" Finnen snaps. "We don't fit."

"You need to loosen up." I tug on the laces of my shirt. "I'm serious, Finn, or this clan business won't work."

His face stills. Then his pale brows draw together. With a soft snarl, he starts undressing.

"Do you have a hard-on for challenges?" I shoot his words back at him and he flinches just a little.

I'm enjoying this, way too much. I like teasing Finnen, and I'm kind of liking the way the Wildman is ripping his few clothes off his body—that ridiculous leather skirt and short boots, laying bare a pale, muscular body that's giving Finnen's a run for its money.

But then Ariadne starts undressing, and all my focus returns to her, all air leaving my lungs.

The guys arouse me with their honed, hard bodies, that

much is the truth, but her soft curves makes me dizzy with desire.

"Here, sweetheart, let me help you." I reach for her and finish the job of ripping her shirt off—fucking finally—to bare her breasts.

And Gods have mercy, they are as juicy and pretty as I'd imagined them to be. As perfect as she is, pale mounds topped with rosy nipples that make my mouth water.

Her eyes drop, lashes dark against the flush in her cheeks, her mouth begging to be kissed, taken, worshipped.

I wonder how long we'll last inside this small, cramped room before we jump each other's bones, before we fall on her like ravenous wolves.

Kiaran makes a noise and I find him with his hand on his hard cock, stroking, gaze fixed on her breasts.

"Fuck." Even Finnen has turned toward us, eyes closed, nostrils flared.

It's her scent, as much as her body, that lights up the room. It fills the small space, intensifying with every breath I draw, and when I glance up at her face, I find her looking at Kiaran and Finnen, her eyes dark like the night.

Then she returns her gaze to me and it snags on my chest, where the laces of my shirt hang loose revealing some of my scars, then it dips to my crotch, and her perfume sharpens.

It's a vicious tug on my balls, and my cock swells, making me grit my teeth.

"Omega," I whisper, "my omega…" Stepping closer, I go to my knees and grab her pants, yank them down, seams and laces ripping, making her yelp. "Mine…"

If she isn't yet in heat, I can't imagine what will happen when she is. The thought loses shape as I bury my face between her legs, her scent making me groan, her slick tasting sweeter than honey on my lips and tongue as I avidly lick at her.

Her hands land on my head, slender fingers digging into my hair, against my scalp. Then, when I lift one of her legs over my shoulders to open her up, she gasps and holds onto my head for balance. I lick at her delicate, wet folds, the small hard nub that makes her moan and tense, the hot opening of her pussy that I stub with the tip of my tongue, making her cry out.

Gods, she's delicious.

Who cares about the food cooling on the trays laid out on the bed when I can feast on her?

When Kiaran appears behind her, I only grunt in vague acknowledgment. He slides his arms around her, cups her breasts, and she starts to come on my tongue, moaning and thrashing.

My fucking Gods... I almost come in my pants as her honey fills my senses, as her pussy contracts against my tongue and she arches back, against Kiaran. She's beautiful as she comes apart.

Damn hot.

I'm kneeling there, dazed, Kiaran still growling deep in his throat, his arms now tight around her, all that's keeping her on her feet, when I realize that Finnen hasn't joined us.

I turn to find him standing naked by the tub, his back to us. I mean, he's blind, but deaf he sure as hell isn't.

"Finn?"

"I thought we were going to bathe," he says.

"Man, are you made of stone or what? Come over here."

Instead of replying, he steps into the tub and sinks down into the hot water. Then he takes the hard bar of soap and starts scrubbing himself, like nothing's amiss.

Yep. He's made of cold marble, for sure, if our little display, if her moans and cries didn't melt the ice in him.

"He wants," Kiaran mutters, and before I can decipher what the hell he's talking about, he grabs Ari, swings her up in her arms. "We all want. So let's fuck."

13

ARIADNE

I'm shaken, shattered by the pleasure Taj thrust into me.

It's certain now, I think. I love having a man's mouth between my legs. My pussy throbs in time to my heart, the pleasure still ebbing through me in gentler waves.

I clutch Kiaran's shoulders, content to be in his arms, skin on warm skin, feeling all that unstoppable strength trapped in his big muscles and hulking frame.

"Such a hussy, wanton woman"—I almost hear the voices of the Temple priestesses in my ear. *"Such a minx, such a tart. A harlot. A trollop."*

But these are my mates.

I am their omega.

And it's taken us forever to get here, where we can get naked and touch, and as Kiaran swings me up in his arms, my only real vague thought is—"Where is Finn?"

"Don't you worry, love." Taj stalks toward the wooden tub, where Kiaran is carrying me at a slower pace—nutmeg-and-cinnamon scent and hot skin stretched over a muscular chest, strong arms around me and blue, blue eyes gazing down at me, filling with darkness as I gaze up at his face. "Finn is just hiding in the tub."

"You could use a good cleaning yourself," Finnen mutters, and I tear my gaze from Kiaran's face to look.

And I look some more, because it's the first time I see Finnen like that, gloriously naked, all strong lines, hard planes and valleys in the clear water, his long hair wet, droplets standing on his shoulders and sculpted chest, and...

"I take my words back," Taj breathes, and I can't look away from Finnen's hard cock that's broken the surface of the water, the plump, flushed head bobbing in front of him as he soaps his muscular arms. "Washing looks good on you, man."

My mouth goes bone-dry. Between the three of them, I'm gone, undone. One of them would be enough to render me speechless. The three of them together are a force of nature, and I want them.

I don't recall ever wanting anything so bad in my life. This craving is consuming me, eating at my thoughts, ruling my body.

But Finnen isn't ready to give in, it seems, unlike me. "You only step into the water if you plan on washing yourselves." He carefully traces the rim of the tub and places the soap there, then soaps his chest. "Fair warning."

"*Fair warning?*" Taj sounds incredulous. "My man, you're rocking a hard-on fit to drill holes through the walls, but you don't want to—?"

"I have my vows," Finnen snaps, "how many times do I need to tell you that—"

"Fuck your vows," Taj says.

"Taj," I reprimand him, but I understand the sentiment. I stare at Finnen. Maybe he will always identify as a priest, always cling to that role.

Kiaran huffs and lowers me into the water, releasing my legs so

I can stand and then sit down in the warmth. He sits on the rim as I gaze at Finnen in front of me. He has stilled, an alabaster marble, tense and stiff—in every sense of the word—across from me.

"Finn?" I whisper. "Do you still have doubts?"

His jaw works, like he wants to speak but can't decide what to say.

"You are both idiots," Kiaran says, glaring at Finnen, then at Taj who's standing beside the tub.

"Me?" Taj growls. "Why the fuck would you say that?"

"So many... obstacles. Reasons, why you shouldn't touch her," Kiaran says. "You said... we're a clan. You said... she is omega. We are alphas. We protect our mate. And we fuck our mate."

"Good speech." Taj's mouth twitches. "Hear that, Finn?"

I sigh. "Guys..."

"You're all obsessed with sex," Finn murmurs.

"You just don't know how to fuck," Taj says, "and it bothers you. You excel at everything else but you're a virgin, aren't you?"

Finnen's cheeks turn crimson. "So what? Don't tell me that he," he nods at Kiaran, "had any sexual experience in the woods? With whom, the jaguars?"

"Fucked by the jaguars," Taj mutters. "Sounds like those sensationalist pamphlets the soldiers like to read."

"What the fuck?" Finnen goes rigid. "Are you serious?"

"About the pamphlets? Sure. Soldiers will read and do anything that will give them a hard-on, and bestiality is a favorite. They—"

"Shut up," Finnen barks.

"Oh, am I offending your sensibilities?"

"Guys!" I splash my hands in the water. "Just... stop!"

And they fall silent.

Now that they have stopped their banter, I don't know what to say.

"Finn..." I whisper. "You can still get out of this bond. You can still go. We haven't sealed this thing between us. You're free to go, you..."

Finnen produces a small noise in the back of his throat, like a strangled groan, and grabs for me in the water. He hauls me onto his lap, and we're splashing water all over the place but I don't care, With a faint moan, I fall against him and when he kisses me, I kiss him back with all I have. His cock is a thick line of fire between our bodies.

"Don't," he whispers against my lips when I pull back for some much-needed air. "Don't set me free. Taj is right, I don't fucking know anything about this. It fucks with my mind."

"What do you want?" I breathe.

"I don't... I want you. I just... don't know how to do this. How to... just be with people." His pale lashes are wet and like dark lace against his cheekbones when he closes his eyes. "The only thing I've known for so fucking long is to fight and pray."

"We'll show you," Taj says softly, and then he's climbing in behind me in the tub, pulling me back against his chest.

"Permission!" Kiaran barks, climbing in behind Finnen.

Finnen jerks forward. "What?"

"Asking for permission to touch," Kiaran says. "Because you want."

"Dammit. Keep your paws to yourself. And promise we'll also teach our Wildman some discretion."

I'm laughing, the sexy moment broken. "Guys."

"First rule of the clan, Finn," Taj says, lifting my wrist to his mouth, licking at my thundering pulse, the scent gland there, "is to accept your desires, stop fighting them."

Finnen mumbles something I don't catch.

"Let's ease him into it," Taj whispers in my ear, making me shiver. His cock is a hard rod at my back. "Touch him. I think that's what he wants the most. And, Kiaran, behave."

Kiaran rumbles a roll of laughter.

"Don't presume to know what I want," Finnen grumbles,

but his cock is still as hard as before, the head bobbing between us, darkened to a near purple. "That's a double-edged sword, and as a military man, you should know. What if I gave you a command—"

Taj groans softly behind me, his cock jumping at my back, and my belly cramps. Even though I just came from his mouth, I need more. I need what I still haven't received. The need to be filled by them is taking over my mind again, and it's inevitable. Inescapable.

I'm naked in the warm water with them, and their scents mingle and surround me, just like their beautiful, strong bodies and lust-dark eyes.

When Taj wraps an arm around my waist and lifts me, when he guides his cock between my legs, I'm ready, so damn ready I almost weep with relief as the head of his cock pushes into me.

"Oh..." My head falls back against Taj's shoulder. "Goddess..."

Finnen groans like he's in pain.

"Want to watch first, priest?" Taj pants as he pushes deeper into me. "See how it's done?"

"Fuck you, I know how—"

Taj thrusts into me and I gasp. "Do you? Watch and learn."

"You know I can't fucking watch!" Finnen snaps, his voice all edges, his control undone.

"Then come closer, priest. Touch. Feel. Listen. Don't you want him to touch you, sweetheart?"

"Yes..." I breathe.

When Finnen leans closer to me, our bodies practically pressed together in the tub, when his hands move over my body, over my breasts, down my belly between my legs where Taj is still sinking deeper and deeper into me, I start to come.

It's a different kind of pleasure than before, slower, bigger, gathering speed as it rolls through me, and Taj grunts, thrusting again, every time sinking a little bit more of that thick rod inside me, and I clench around it, again and again, a cry escaping me.

"Goddamn," Taj manages, and then his cock is jerking inside me, Finnen's fingers playing around Taj's cock, teasing and rubbing, and the avalanche smothers me as I come, clenching so hard inside that a cry escapes me. I grab Finnen's shoulders so that I can ride Taj's cock, lifting myself a little only to slam back down, and it's so big he still isn't fully inside me. It burns and it hurts, but it feels too good to stop. Taj's hands are leaving bruises on my ribs, on my hips as he takes his pleasure, growling something resembling my name in my ear. His cock is like a fist inside me now, so big I can hardly bear it, and yet it's perfect, exactly what I need.

More pleasure rolls through me, almost too much, and I slow my movements, shuddering.

Vaguely aware that Finnen scrambles out of the tub, splashing water all over, a panicky look on his face.

That Kiaran is stroking his cock lazily, eyes half-lidded, leaning back across from me in the tub.

That Taj's muscular body is trembling at my back, his breath coming in hot wheezes on my neck, his cock still jerking inside of me.

I'm stunned, in shock, still unable to comprehend that I have a man's cock inside of me, that it feels so right, so good, that it can give me so much astonishing pleasure.

Noy a virgin anymore, I think, and it's half-shame and half-pride that fills me.

Even if the voices still crowd my head, calling me a whore and all the things I've heard over my years at the Temple about omegas—bitches in heat, sex-addicts, nymphomaniacs—who cares?

I'm sure my mind will catch up at some point and show me that I do care, that I'm confused, but I'm getting used to this alternate reality where I crave these men, where my body knows what it's good for it. For me.

Because I'm shaking, too, shaking with the rightness of it, of some deep need in me finally met, and all I know is that now it won't stop. It won't let me go.

Now I need more.

14

ARIADNE

"You okay, sweetheart?" Taj's voice in my ear startles me, rouses me. "Did sex with me knock you out?"

With a huff, I struggle to sit up, lifting my head off his padded shoulder, but his grip on my hips tightens.

"Did I hurt you?" he breathes. "I realize that for a first time, the tub and this position weren't the best. I apologize for that, though I won't apologize for fucking you. I'll never regret that."

"I'm okay, I just..." I hiss a little when my movements jostle his cock inside me. It's softer than it was before, but it's still big and I feel bruised inside. "It was good."

"That's all?" He huffs a laugh. "Didn't I manage to blow your mind?"

I try again to get off him and this time he helps me with a muttered curse. I moan when he slowly pulls out of me. I turn my head to look at him and smile.

"I loved it, Taj."

His frown smooths out and he grins at me. "You did, huh?"

I nod and glance over at Kiaran who is still lazily stroking himself. The plump head of his cock is flushed dark, and every time it appears over his big fist, I feel an answering throb down below. His head has fallen back against the rim of the wooden tub. Washed clean of most of the grime, his chest gleams like white marble, all chiseled lines and smooth planes, a dark scar on his left arm, another on a muscular thigh.

My pussy throbs. My core clenches painfully. My breath comes in short gasps.

"Kia..." Goddess, he looks like a fallen god, water droplets glistening on his trimmed beard, on his flushed cheekbones and pale lashes. His tresses trail in the water.

"I want you," he says, "now," and releasing his cock, he grabs my arms and drags me through the water over to him.

I fall against his chest with a yelp, and his mouth crashes on mine before I can catch my breath, his hands going to my ass. His fingers slide between my legs and push into me, relentless, not giving respite.

Fucking me in hard strokes where I ache and burn and want.

Giving something but not all of what I crave.

Slowly, he pulls his fingers out, making me whimper, sucking on my lower lip and lifting those two fingers to his nose to smell them.

A groan escapes him.

I need him. I rub my face against his bearded cheek, drawing in his scent, needing to smear it all over me.

"Ariadne," he breathes, his voice rough. His eyes dip to my breasts, my nipples hard and aching. They pucker more under his gaze. "I fucking want you."

"Yes," I whisper. "Yes, please..."

His cock bobs between our bodies. I put my hands on it, close my fingers around its fat girth, and he leans back, softly groaning. I play with it, explore its shape, its hardness.

I lift up on my knees in the water, straddling him, rubbing

his cock against my belly, drawing in an uneven breath when it swells more, a vein beating under the silky skin. It moves in my hands with a life of its own.

His stomach muscles tighten, his neck arches back, and he mumbles a vicious curse.

Then with a grunt, he's shoving me back against Taj and lifting one of my legs over his shoulder, and already he's entering me, grunting, his gaze fixed where he's thrusting into me, and...

I'm coming again, my breath knocked out of me, my body tightening around his big cock, rippling, my core clenching so hard tears leak from my eyes.

Goddess, yes...

Taj mutters my name and his hands slide around me to cup my breasts, his callused fingers on my nipples, rubbing and tugging. I'm still coming, gasping and rocking on Kiaran's cock. He's growling, a feral expression on his handsome face, blue eyes turned almost black with desire, pale locks brushing his jaw with every savage thrust. He has one hand on my leg, keeping it folded over his shoulder, and the raw, naked lust on his face has me moaning, clenching again.

Kiaran groans my name, snarls, fucks me harder, shoving me against Taj until he's almost on top of both of us. Taj's hard cock is nudging at my ass, and his breaths are coming faster in my ear. He's rubbing the tips of my nipples and I never imagined it could feel so delicious, that every tug of his fingers on the sensitive nubs would translate to a rush of pleasure between my legs, where I'm still rippling around Kiaran's cock.

Kiaran grabs the rib of the tub, hunching over me, his locks swinging, brushing my arms, more points of sensation on my over-sensitized skin, a low, guttural sound leaving his lips. His cock pulses inside me, spilling fire, and I'm burning.

Between two of my men, filled with one's cock, the other's

hands on my breasts, I feel a contentment unlike any I've ever felt in my life—especially these past days, since leaving the fort, with all that unrequited lust I had to suffer through.

But it's not enough, because someone is missing.

"Finn," I whisper. "Where is Finn?"

"Hey, priest," Taj says and the quality of his voice makes me glance around the room, not sure what I'm supposed to be seeing.

"You're rutting like animals," Finn breathes, but it's not anger I hear in his voice. It's something else. "I fucking can't... oh Gods, fuck..."

Kiaran pulls out of me, hissing, then falls back in the water, a stunned expression on his face that fades into sleepiness, a lazy grin spreading on his face. At any other time, I'd snicker. He looks like a sated cat who lapped up all the cream and is now licking his whiskers, damn proud of himself.

But... *Finnen.*

I put my hands over Taj's. He's still rock hard at my back and he grunts when I shift against him. Slowly, I pull his hands off my breasts and he trails them down to my waist.

He lets out a strangled breath. "Fuck..."

I know he's staring at Finnen, as I am. I think the only one of us unaware of what is going on outside the tub is Kiaran whose eyes have drifted closed. He looks passed out, head lolling on the wooden rim, not seeing Finnen.

Finnen who is on the bed where all the clothing was heaped, his back to the wall, his hand on his cock. His long white hair is dripping on the covers, his face is flushed, his mouth slack as he works his cock in frantic, harsh motions. I take him in, every hard, strong line of his body and face, cast in pale stone just like Kiaran, muscles honed from years of endless practice and ritual. He has a dark patch on one of his muscular thighs. Is it a bruise?

And his cock... Gods above, it's as big as it has felt against me before, and now it's bared, long and thick and dripping wet, his fist making an obscene squelching sound as it slides up and down his length. His eyes are half-closed, but they are fixed on me.

On us.

As if he can see us.

Not possible, right?

And right now, all I can see is him. Never seen my priest so debauched, so out of control. So openly aroused and giving in to his desire.

Excitement unfurling again in my belly, I climb out of the tub and walk over to him, leaving wet footprints, small puddles of water behind. I've never thought much of my body, a tool for the rituals of the goddess, fit to do what it must do every day at the Temple. Never thought it beautiful or desirable, never considered my breasts as anything but encumberment, never thought of my curves as something others might enjoy.

But Finnen groans, and his eyes seem to rove over me.

"Finn?" I come to stand in front of him and he tilts his head back a little, eyes still fixed on me. The dark patch on his thigh looks like scales, like the patch Taj has on his back. I open my mouth to ask him about it, slightly distracted away from the sight of the rest of him, but he chooses that moment to speak.

"I see you," he breathes, and I go very still.

"What do you mean?"

"In battle and arousal, I see you. I see things, outlines, but now... now I see more. More of you."

He can see me. The thought makes every part of me clench. My nipples tighten and my breasts feel heavier as I lean over him, as I get on the bed between his spread legs on my knees.

And his eyes dip where my breasts hang, one hand lifting to cup one, his thumb brushing over my nipple. His breath catches.

"Look at the both of you," Taj says from behind me,

startling me. "That hard-on looks painful. How long has it been since you've allowed yourself to come? You have a chronic case of blue balls, I'll bet."

Finnen growls. "Shut up."

"Taj," I start, warningly.

"Then again, you've probably never spent weeks being hard all the fucking time," Taj continues, thoughtfully. "You're unlike any alpha I've ever heard of."

"You are hard," Kiaran growls, coming to stand by the bed, a grin on his face. His cock is bobbing in front of him, already hardening again. "Permission!"

"Dammit," Finnen mutters, but his cock twitches. "I can see all of you. Talk about being hard..."

Taj chuckles and reaches down to stroke himself. "So you can see this, huh? Take a good look, then. It's both for Ariadne and you, priest."

"It's that supposed to please me?" Finn grunts, but his cheeks flush a deeper red. His thumb flicks over my nipple again, making me gasp.

"Do you even know what to do with all that cock?" Taj slings an arm over Kiaran's shoulders, who stiffens and jerks a little. "Is it time for your first lesson in sex?"

"Fuck you," Finnen barks.

"Thanks, but don't distract me. I'm trying to help you, man."

"With what?"

"Pleasuring a woman."

A shiver runs through me when Finnen's white gaze returns to me. His hand is so big, engulfing my breast.

"What should I do?" Finnen whispers, and for the first time since I met him, he sounds uncertain.

"Okay, lesson one," Taj says, and Kiaran huffs, still leaning slightly away from Taj who's enthusiastically hanging off him. "This goes for you, too, Wildman, so pay attention. Fucking our girl fast and hard can be good, if she's into it, and with the preheat she's pretty wet, so... that works, but to give her more pleasure, you need to know what feels good for her, and it's not always your cock."

Finnen splutters a little, the flush spreading over his chest. He looks about to self-combust. "Will you get to the point?"

"Before you come just from the sound of my voice? Sure. Men and women, alphas and omegas, we are built from the same building blocks. Where you like to be touched, she likes it too. See what I mean?"

Finnen grunts.

"Use your fingers," Taj goes on. "Touch her where she's wet, between her legs. Yeah?"

I moan when Finnen's other hand travels between my thighs, stroking, spreading me. His breathing grows choppy, and so does mine.

"Feel her?" Taj's voice is turning hoarse. "How wet and hot she is down there? Stroke up and down, between her folds, feel every part of her. Feel her opening, and that small nub at the top. Feel it?"

I shudder when Finnen's finger skims over the nub before slipping in my slick and brushing over my opening. He rocks upward, his hips restless, his hard cock bumping against my stomach, leaving behind a hot smear of precum.

"Play with the nub," Taj instructs, and helplessly I glance sideways at him and Kiaran and find them both stroking their hard cocks. Gah, what a view... "Circle it with your finger, rub it just the way you are rubbing her nipple."

And Finnen does just that, wrenching a moan from my throat. I can't help but rock against his hand a little, feeling my belly tighten with arousal.

Goddess, hearing Taj describe what Finn is doing to me, what he plans on doing...

And having Finn follow the orders, the directions, feeling

his cock jump again and again against my belly, hearing his muffled groans, it's adding fuel to the fire burning inside me.

"Now," Taj says, his voice breathless, "slip a finger inside her. Feel how tight she is, how damn hot... Gods dammit..."

Kiaran growls something, the sounds of them both jerking off rude and filthy and erotic.

Finnen's finger dips into me, thick and rough, and it's so good but not enough. I rock on it, panting, needing more.

"Add another finger," Taj instructs. "And another. As many as she can take."

Oh Goddess...

Two more fingers slide into me, stretching me, and at any other time it would be painful but after taking the others' cocks in me, it's just right. When I clench around his fingers, Finnen bares his teeth, body arching, his cock twitching and jerking against my belly.

He's so beautiful.

And I cry out as my entire body tightens at the sight and feel of him, at this vulnerable side of him, his desire to pleasure me, the way it feeds into his own.

I don't even react when Taj and Kiaran move behind me and come all over my back with loud grunts, painting it with their cum, because all I can see right now, riding the waves of my orgasm, is Finnen finding his own pleasure.

He's still thrusting his fingers inside me, but the movement has become jerky and jagged, his cock thick and hot against my belly. Arching up, he rubs it up and down, eyes shut, lips parted, his other hand a fist in the bedcovers. Back and forth, rubbing his swollen erection over my slick skin, groans rumbling from his chest, pale hair spread around his head, glinting like silver in the flickering light of the oil lamp.

Suddenly, he lets out a long moan, like a wounded animal, and his cock spasms, spewing cum all over my breasts, my neck, even my chin. His gaze follows the trail and he comes again, another spurt that crisscrosses over the first one.

"Gods," he pants, his powerful body relaxing finally against the mattress, his head rolling back, his fingers slipping out of me, his cock shrinking between our bodies. "Oh Gods…"

If he was beautiful before, now he's breathtaking.

I hope the gods are watching.

15

FINNEN

The evening passes in lapses of time, scenes as if described in a book. It's as if it's someone else's life I'm observing, not mine. I feel detached, floating somewhere in a corner of the ceiling, looking down at this group of people in the small, poorly lit room. Three men, one of them looking like me lying on his back on the bed, a pretty girl over him, and his face rapt as he comes, losing all control, all sense of propriety, breaking all vows.

The relief is indescribable.

The shame hasn't left me entirely—I'm not the kind of man to change his views in the blink of an eye—but the doubts have retreated to another corner, far from me.

My omega, I think. She's mine. They are all mine, these people in the room.

My mind is starting to harmonize with my body. All that rigid discipline is mostly physical, tactile memory, and now I'm replacing it with pleasure, with real human touch, and I could fucking cry at how good it feels.

Snap, snap.

I'm lying on the bed, staring blindly up at the ceiling, tears in my eyes I fucking refuse to let fall.

Her scent is all over me, everywhere, warm and sweet, and now I've found my release... comforting.

But then the scene snaps to the guys pulling me off the bed and back to the bath. The water is tepid but as Taj pushes me to sit down in it, Kiaran is lowering Ariadne across from me, her scent giving her away, and I'm confused as to what they might want.

I can't see her anymore, and it saddens me, but then hands brush over my arms and a wet washcloth is run over me. Another comfort I'm not used to, as Taj cleans me up from sweat and filth, from my cum and her slick.

My head falls back against the rim of the tub.

Is this really me? Floating on a cloud of calm and pleasure, muscles held tight too long relaxing, my limbs growing heavy as lead. Soft splashing tells me that Kiaran must be cleaning her the same way, and her leg brushes against mine, sending a jolt of renewed awareness through me.

My cock valiantly tries to rally and harden, but my body isn't up to this.

I almost laugh at the pun.

At the madness.

At the rightness of it.

Maybe I doze off. Maybe I pass the fuck out, I don't know. The only time I recall ever passing out was when I fell during ritual practice when I was younger and cracked my head on the floor.

But then reality returns and I'm out of the water and wrapped in a bath sheet, a bowl of stew in my lap, a cup of ale beside me. The stew is good. Everything is good right now—the warmth, the food, the company. After spending all my life priding myself on thriving in a hostile, cold world, a dark world at that, I'm finding it hard to let go of the self-control that kept me alive, but with these men and this girl...

Yeah, with them, maybe it's okay to let go for a while, allow myself to tear down some of the walls and rest.

We eat like wolves, dress like humans in the clothes left on the bed, and sleep like the dead, two in each bed. What are we, though? It seems we can't deny the Fae blood in us any longer, even though we pretend that nothing has changed.

Everything has changed.

I end up with Kiaran, one arm thrown over me and I find I don't mind when I turn in the night on my side. When I gasp awake from a familiar nightmare, one that has haunted me since I was a child, all mixed up with my parents' death that I haven't witnessed, through in the dream I am there, unable to help, failing them... I don't mind when he pulls me closer to him until I fall back asleep.

And there's another snap of the thread of time, because next thing I know, I'm waking up. Correction, something has woken me up.

Outside the small window with its leather panes, I think I hear rain pattering. A rooster somewhere crows the dawn of a new day.

Something is off, though I can't put my finger on it.

It's probably the lack of tension in my body, the floaty feeling that persists, reeling in memories from last night, memories that make me want to grin.

So unbecoming of a priest. Even a banished, sentenced one.

Taj and Ariadne are already up, talking quietly with one another, my hearing snatching words like "long way" and "provisions" and "careful." Not hard to guess that the topic is our journey and its dangers.

I think they're munching on something, too, probably left-over bread from last night, and my stomach grumbles at the thought. I recall slurping stew and eating hard bread before memory faded out again, but it feels like years have passed. I start to sit up, see if they left anything for us to breakfast on, when strong arms wrap around me, keeping me down.

A rough male voice says in my ear, "Permission?"

And I elbow him in the stomach. "For fuck's sake!" I turn a glare on Kiaran, because I know his voice, and his scent, and fuck, his touch. "You're becoming worse than Taj."

"Why, because I touch?" He pokes a finger at my arm. "Touch you."

"I didn't give you permission." I grab his poking finger and lift it off me. "You ask for permission and wait for it before you start, get it?"

He's quiet and still, the only sound his breathing. His hand twists in mine, clasping my fingers. "Trust, Finnen."

Nonplussed, my own breath catching, I wait to see what he will do. In the dark, light flashes as my body prepares for something—combat or sex, either seems to stress me enough for that.

But he keeps holding my hand, saying nothing, until the lights fade.

"Morning, Finn." Ariadne's voice sends a pleasant shiver down my spine, and fuck, I'm getting hard. Just from that.

"Trust," Kiaran says again and I pull my hand away, fucking confused.

"Trust you?" I ask. "Is that what you mean?"

"Trust that I stop." His voice is serious, earnest. "If you say no."

I nod, run my hands over my face. My heart is slowing down, my muscles still quivering.

"Relax," Taj says, "and come eat something, the both of you."

For the first time, I don't send him to the hells, but nod again, instead.

Maybe he's right, after all. Last night is a pleasant dream

and I smile when I think about it. Maybe it's okay to relax. Stay relaxed. We made it this far. Soon we will officially be on our way to the south, and there we will be safe.

Our omega will be safe.

Everything is going to be fucking all right.

———

The bread is stale but it calms the hunger in my stomach. Some left over ale makes my head buzz. Above all, the quiet, the simple act of sitting together under a roof and eating and drinking is fucking with my head.

In a good way.

A *new* way that has me second-guessing my every move.

Kiaran elbows me at some point and laughs, and I don't know why, but my mouth twitches.

"What?"

"You relax."

"Yeah, yeah. Trying." I swallow the rest of my ale to buy myself time. Being around Kiaran is like having a puppy—a big, strong, sexy puppy—and the thought almost makes me choke on the ale.

Relaxing doesn't mean I'll turn into Taj and fuck everything in sight, right?

Good thing I can't see.

"Tell us," I say to hide my slight unease, "what did you decide about our journey south? Can we buy provisions here?"

"Probably," Taj says. "We'll have to see if the innkeeper is still in a good mood. I mean, we weren't that loud, were we?"

Heat rushes over my skin. I open my mouth but no sound emerges.

Dammit.

"The clothes fit us," Ariadne says. "Taj still has coin, enough to buy food for the way, maybe a blanket or two.

We'll pass through the town, buy what we can, and be on our way."

"You're afraid the Temple might recognize us," I say.

"Aren't you?"

I shrug. "Many things could go wrong."

"Such an optimist," Taj says. "What about you, Kiaran? What do you think? It's a straightforward plan, isn't it?"

"You are coming with us, Kia, aren't you?" Ariadne whispers. "Have you made up your mind?"

I had forgotten that Kiaran was with us only temporarily, until he decided what to do.

When he doesn't reply, the knot in my stomach tightens. I thought that was set, I thought this group was tight. I let my guard down last night with them, but he's still unsure?

Resisting an urge to grab and shake him, I stuff my mouth with the last bit of bread. "We need to reach Stalia or Tarcsto before the snows."

"I thought winter would be milder down south," Ariadne says.

"It is." Taj chews loudly. Probably with his mouth open, the uncouth bastard. "But there are marshes and they freeze just enough to let you wander over them only to suck you in at unsuspected moments."

"Have you traveled all over the Empire?"

"No, but I've been to the south, twice, on two separate campaigns. If we manage to cross over here"—he places a cup down on the floor with a small thump—"and reach Stalia, as you say, before the marshes freeze over, we stand a good chance of continuing down, maybe by boat if we manage, to Pise or Sutri."

"Are those towns pro-Fae?" Ariadne asks quietly. She sounds worried. Probably as much about the journey as about Kiaran's lack of response.

"They were last I heard," I say. I think of my parents' last message, a few months ago, which used the code we had always used to say that things hadn't changed. "The cities in the Rising Moon Lands are Fae-friendly."

Not a written message. Obviously. They had sent me seeds in a small pouch.

I planted them in the garden of the Temple, in a small town close to the Summer Capital. That before the Unnamed god spoke to me and I made the mistake of listening.

Or so I thought until recently. A mistake. An error in judgment. A loss of self-control. But that mistake led me to Ariadne. To them.

To this clan, this bond.

"Finn? Finn!" Taj sounds like he's been calling my name for a while.

Instinctively, I turn the tables on him, attacking instead of retreating. You attack or you're eaten alive inside the Temple. "How did you become a commander this young? What did you do?"

"Are you... what, doubting me?"

"Doubting you?" I say. "Now that's interesting. Why would I?"

Taj is silent for a long moment and at first, I think he won't answer and I'll have to say something snide just to prod him.

But then he says, "I made a mistake."

It's as if he's echoing my thoughts. "Explain yourself. What sort of a mistake? Run away from the enemy, did you? Or wait, I got it. You were ordered to do something and that gave you such a hard-on you couldn't walk."

Here I go, my sarcastic self in full display, and after last night, I should put that side of me away, lock it inside a box and bury it in the ground, but it's a part of who I am now. Might as well bury myself.

He doesn't even seem to notice what I said.

"I saved the General, during a campaign in the south," he says quietly."

"That's a big mistake," I mutter.

"My mistake was that I didn't die."

———

"Saving the General was a noble act," Ariadne says as we leave the small room where I had such a revelation, trooping down the stairs one by one. "It's no wonder they promoted you, Taj."

"A campaign in the south." I'm gripping the rail, shuffling my feet one at a time as I go down the stairs last. Stairs are terrifying even for seeing people, let alone blind old me. "You were after the Fae-bloods."

His silence is answer enough.

"You saved the General and he captured people, sent them to the Central capital," I go on, following the thought.

"I was a soldier," he says harshly. "I followed orders. I was a cog in the machine."

"Easy to say."

"Easy?" He's waiting for me as I climb off the last step. "Really, that's what you think? I had no choice. It was many years ago. How old do you think I am? What choices do you think I had as an abandoned child taken in by the army, a squire following the troops?"

"Fuck." I nod, sigh. "Okay."

"*Okay*? That's all you have to say?"

"Yes. *Okay*, Taj. I'm starting to see your point, all right?"

He harrumphs. "Let's get going. Here's Skotos."

The clopping of hooves answers my question before it leaves my lips.

"You named your horse," I say.

"Yeah, imagine that, even a black-hearted Fae-killing thug like me can name his horse. Come, Skot!"

He's furious at me and at any other time, I'd have given back as good as I got, but right now all I feel is a sense of the ground giving way under my feet.

I rush after them, not sure what else I can say. All my beliefs, my credos, are being overturned one by one, and I can't catch up. It's all dark around me, in me, an unknown, a chasm so deep I've never felt so sure I'll fall to my death before.

When I stumble, I fully expect to tumble headfirst into the abyss, but strong hands steady me.

"Careful," Kiaran growls, and then Ariadne slips an arm around me.

"You can lean on us sometimes, you know," she whispers.

Still panicky, I let them take me out of the inn. Is this what being with others, having feelings for others is like? Losing that snark and bite that kept me going, that kept me alive all these years? Is that a good thing?

This... relaxing part?

Still not sold on it.

I shake Kiaran off the moment we clear the entrance of the inn and he skulks off, grumbling under his breath. Having Ariadne by my side feels less like I'm a useless blind man and more like I'm walking with my girl.

Her soft snort of laughter lets me know she knows exactly what I'm thinking, but I'm still dazed and don't give a damn if anyone thinks me weak for it and mocks me.

"You're something, Finn," she breathes, and there you have it.

"All of us are something," I mutter.

"But you're the strongest of us."

I almost miss a step. "How do you figure that?"

She tsks and rests her head on my shoulder, not giving me a reply.

"It's not true," I say. "I'm the weakest link in this clan. I'm blind, for fuck's sake."

"But inside, you're steel. You know what is important. What you need."

My turn to snort, because those days are long gone. I wonder if I ever did know. In any case, right now I'm lost, and seeing the others' confidence in bed and with each other, I feel like a mole who's been pulled out to the light for the first time in his life.

And he's still blind, only now it matters, where it didn't matter in the dark before. When you live and breathe darkness, when you don't know the light, you don't miss anything, but once you've been out of your hole in the ground, that airless, suffocating passage that doubled as your tomb?

It changes everything.

———

The feeling of wrongness persists as we walk through the streets, between tall houses that echo our steps and the clopping of Skotos' hooves. Then again, Taj is mad at me and funny how something that mattered naught to me not so long ago now has me twisted up in knots.

It seems that relaxing parts of you held tense and rigid for most of your life—and I am referring to my mind rather than other rigid parts of me, thank you very fucking much—isn't easy.

That forming relationships with people that go beyond saying hello in the morning and nodding as you cross paths with them is much more complex than I ever thought.

Also pleasurable, my mind provides and I shush it.

I have enough confusion plaguing me as it is, without a constant reminder of last night's activities.

Ariadne leaning over me, her breasts heavy, nipples hard, her scent wrenching at me, my cock brushing over her belly...

Dammit.

I'm hard, and the fact that Taj hasn't noticed and teased me about it leaves an ache in my gut. Kiaran is walking ahead with him, and I need to do something. Bridge this suddenly bothersome chasm. Having Ariadne pressed to my side counts for a lot, but I need the others, too.

Talk about suddenly realizing all the things. The thought of going on without them, without their respect, their appreciation, would hurt like a damn wound to the chest.

"Taj!" I call out. "Wait."

"What do you want, Finn?" he says without stopping. "I feel guilty enough without your help."

"I wasn't going to accuse you of anything," I say.

"That's a refreshing change."

Wow, would you look at that. Taj is giving me a run for my money in the sarcasm department. He's furious.

I sigh. "Are you more upset with me or with yourself right now?"

"I knew it. I knew you would pass the blame back to me. Fuck you, Finn."

"Taj," Ariadne says. "Wait for us."

"Taj!" Kiaran barks. "Slow down!"

And then the sound of a small scuffle alerts me to the fact that Kiaran has grappled Taj to stop him, and I can't help a smile.

"Damn it, Wildman, let go of me or I'll punch you in the face," Taj warns even as his voice approaches us.

"Look," I say, "I just wanted to say I'm sorry, okay?"

"What was that?" Taj huffs. "I didn't hear you. Would you repeat that?"

"Damn you, Taj. Sorry okay? I'm only starting to get to know you, only starting to understand... lots of stuff." Ariadne's scent, her arm around me gives me the strength to keep talking. "I want to learn more about you. About all of you. Give me a chance, okay?"

Taj lets out a shuddering breath. "Deal, priest. Keep an open mind and we'll do that. We'll have plenty of time on our way south."

My stomach roils, the bad feeling returning, worse. Why? I groan a little and Ariadne's arm tightens around my back.

"Are you all right, Finn?" she asks softly.

"I'm fine. Let's keep moving. Where is Kiaran?"

"Kia!" Ariadne pulls away from my side. "Where is he going?"

Oh fuck. I'm going to throw up. What the fuck is wrong with me? It's as if a dark cloud is gathering inside my head.

"Wildman! Come here. You dragged me back to talk to Finnen, now it's your turn." Taj grunts, curses.

"Take your hands... fuck... off me..." Kiaran shoves at Taj, and by now lights are flashing in my vision, painting their outlines, my heart beating a staccato like a Temple drum in my chest. "I'm going."

"Going where? What's going on?" I breathe.

"I don't know!" Ariadne moves further from me. "Kiaran, what's wrong?"

"This town." Kiaran is panting, a sharp quality to his voice I've never heard before. "I remember it. I know it."

"What are you talking about?" Taj grunts again. "Stop it, man, where are you gonna go, huh? What are you gonna do?"

"I know it. There's a house..." Kiaran's voice fades a little, grows distant. "A house."

"What fucking house?"

"He's from this town," I mutter. "He probably grew up here before he showed signs of Fae blood and his parents abandoned him in the hills."

"Oh no." Ariadne sounds upset, and Taj is cursing again, but something else draws my attention away from them.

There's a sound... It echoes in the town and I can't pinpoint it.

Sounds like a horse... a horse galloping.

I turn. Then turn the other way. Where is it coming from? My heart is pounding hard against my ribs, my breaths echo in my ears. I'm damn dizzy.

It's riders.

Riders are coming down the street.

Toward us.

"Hide!" I yell at the others. "Hide, now! Take Ariadne away!"

"Finn," Taj starts.

"Take her now!"

"But you—"

I break into a sprint, running toward the riders. I somehow know that they are either Temple or military, that they spotted us, somehow recognized us.

"Finn, no!" Ariadne screams but I don't stop—instead running faster, harder, straight at the galloping horses.

Someone shouts an order, the horses slow down, and I'm still racing toward them, each breath a slice through my lungs, my boots catching on cobblestones but still I manage not to fall.

I have to distract the riders.

Give my clan a chance to flee or hide.

I have to stop them.

I have to—

The hooves thunder so fucking close to me, a sharp pebble cuts a line of fire on my cheek—and then hands grab me, lift me in the air.

I howl.

I'm thrown belly-first on a saddle and the horse canters away, while a voice says, "Find them!"

16

ARIADNE

Kiaran is dragging me into a side street, behind a cart with a hay-chomping mule harnessed to it, cursing under his breath. Taj is right behind us, clothes flying as he races to catch up with us.

"Finn!" I gasp. "Where is Finn?"

"Shush." And for good measure, Kiaran slaps a big hand over my mouth. "Hide. Finn say hide."

"We left him there?" I shout behind his hand but nothing intelligible comes out. I try to pull his hand away. "Finn!"

Taj reaches us as Kiaran pulls me down to the ground, behind the cart. "Good thought. Stay down."

I bite at Kiaran's fingers, tasting salt, and he releases me, giving me a startled look. I draw a deep breath, trying to fill my aching chest.

"Finn," he says quietly. "Where?"

"They were so damn fast!" Taj pants, crouching down beside me, dark hair falling in his eyes. "The riders grabbed him as they passed, took him away."

"No!" I breathe.

"That idiot. He ran straight at them."

"Why would he do that, why—?"

"To distract them, give us a chance to save ourselves. If they kill him, I'll find him and kill him again myself."

"You're not making any sense!" I whisper-shout.

He's rubbing at his chest. "That damned, cute idiot. I'll spank him when I see him again. And fuck, our horse has run off. We're on foot now."

"Were they of the Temple?" I ask. "Did they recognize him?"

"The colors were military," Taj says somberly. "It was me they recognized. They must have been told I may be traveling with a group."

"That inn-keeper," I hiss. "She blabbed at someone about you."

"Yeah. Beware friendly, nice people. Damn."

"What now? How do we find him and get him back? We can't leave him with them!"

"Of course not," Taj says and that tugs on a spiky shard of panic that's been digging into my chest, pulling it out, calming me down a little. "We'll get him back."

"Where would they take him?"

"The Summer Capital," Taj says and the words settle over me like a shroud, heavy and oppressing. "Eremis."

Shit. We were going to avoid the capital, where they're waiting to execute us.

"We were supposed to teach him how to fuck," Taj mutters. "We can't let him die a virgin. I prepared a curriculum for him and Kiaran."

"A what?" I'm terrified and my heart is trying to pound its way out of my chest and what the hell is he talking about?

"Materials, lessons for them."

"Goddess, Taj, can we focus on the task at hand?"

"Yeah, we need to move away from this cart and hide somewhere better until we can flee this shitty town and... Kiaran? Where the fuck are you going, man? Come back here."

"Kiaran!" I yell-whisper. "Where are you going?"

To my relief, he stops, turns back. His pale locks swing forward to shadow his face. At least he's half-hidden in the shadow of the house porch with its two square pillars. The expression on his face is strange.

"Kia." I reach out a hand to him. "Come back. We have to decide what to do."

"My family is here," he says.

For a long moment I wonder if I misheard. "Your family?"

Am I hearing things? Is this what shock does to you?

"My family." He thumps a fist on his chest, brows drawing together. "Here."

"Makes sense," Taj mutters. "It's the closest town to the hills where we found him. This would be the place, if it wasn't one of the villages. Finnen guessed it right." He nods at Kiaran. "And so what? You gonna ask them to take you back? Nothing has changed. You're an alpha. Your ears remain pointed and I bet somewhere on your body you have the scales of Fae blood."

I frown. "I'd have noticed those scales by now, wouldn't I? And what about me? Do I have scales anywhere?"

"On females, they're supposed to be very fine," Taj mutters, his gaze still fixed on Kiaran, "and pale, and sometimes only show once they are with child."

With child. My thoughts wrap around that image, sending a violent shiver down my spine—apprehension and excitement and panic and joy—when Kiaran turns away again and starts walking.

"Dammit," Taj hisses, then he's on his feet and reaching down for me. "Come on. Looks like the Wildman wants to introduce us to his family. So romantic, isn't he?"

———

Romantic or not, we have to jog to keep up with his big strides, and he never slows down, leading us through narrow streets and alleys. I keep glancing over my shoulder, in case more riders appear to take us away, but there's no sound of hooves, just voices, coughs, babies wailing and dogs yowling. Distantly, a cart rattles down a main street.

Incongruously, birds chirp in the half-hidden gardens of the houses we pass by as we rush along, not sure where we're going and what Kiaran wants to do.

I can't forget the fact he hasn't yet said anything about staying with us, and though I trust him—he's saved our lives a few times already—I don't know what his plan is.

What he hopes to do.

Whether he's thinking rationally or if it's an emotional pull he feels toward the family who abandoned him. I can't blame him, honestly. Emotion has always governed me, no matter how I tried to shed all feeling and become Artume's perfect vessel.

They say the Fae were always governed by violent passions. The chroniclers spent a lot of pages on their depravity and fury, their violence and bloody taking of revenge, their ardent love for their own and their unrepentant defense of it.

I'm starting to think that I could never have made a good vessel, a good priestess of a virgin goddess. A human goddess. That giving in to my emotions isn't a sin, that this is how I was meant to be.

And that Kiaran is no different, much more so because he was never taught to suppress his emotions, to control himself like the rest of us were. So unlike Taj's military discipline and worse even, Finnen's Temple training.

Goddess, Finn... The thought of him as a prisoner and carried away from us is an open wound in my chest. What if they hurt him? What if they killed him?

No, I can't even consider the possibility, and—

We almost stumble into Kiaran who has stopped suddenly in a narrow street, lined with well-kept two-story houses, their cloistered balconies beautifully carved from dark wood, their porticos arched and columnated.

Only the house Kiaran is standing in front of is...

"Fire," he whispers. "Burn."

"Yeah," Taj mutters, "this house is burned down all right. Burned to ashes. Wait... is this your house? Dammit, Kiaran."

"Did your family die in a fire?" I whisper, remembering his reaction to the burning meat back at his cave. "Oh goddess, I'm so sorry."

"No." He blinks. "Cousins."

"This is your *cousins'* house?" I ask.

"I'm confused," Taj says.

"You were sent here to live with your cousins," I whisper, "and someone burned them? But you escaped."

"They carried me," he says. "Away. Left me."

"The townsfolk?"

He scowls at the burnt ruins. "Family."

"What? But—"

"Aunt. Uncle."

"Oh. Shit. More family, huh?" Taj scowls. "Such nice people."

"They help us. Now. They help us."

"Really. Why would they?"

"Exchange," he says, a slow grin spreading on his face, baring too many teeth, and canines that are too sharp to be human. "For their lives."

———

"This isn't a good idea," I mutter as we follow Kiaran down the street to where presumably the rest of his family live. I feel... weird. Heat flows through me, making sweat bead on my skin, waves of it. I'm hot and cold and hot again, and my belly is cramping—a different pain from before, but still present enough for me to take notice.

"I mean," Taj says, "what do we have to lose? We need to leave this town quickly. If they can hide us for the day, give us horses and food, we can be out of here by nightfall."

"We are going to threaten them. And hope they don't manage to grab us instead and deliver us to the army or the Temple."

"We'll get the drop on them."

"You sound so sure we can do this. Is it so easy for you to force people?"

"Remember they abandoned Kiaran," Taj growls, "*our* Kiaran when he was a little child, out in the wilderness to die. It's a fucking miracle he survived. Don't go feeling pity for them now."

"You're right," I whisper. Morals are all fine and good until you remember what sort of people you're dealing with. *Oof...* More heat washes through me, and my belly clenches.

"Are you okay?" Taj asks.

"Too hot."

"Sex can bring on your heat faster."

"Couldn't you have said so earlier?"

"Would that have made a difference?"

No. He's right. It's a vicious circle. I want sex, and sex is bringing my heat closer, which only makes me want more sex.

"Here," Kiaran says and stops in front of another house— not a burned down one this time, but a perfectly fine, perfectly tall and...

"Gods dammit," Taj breathes, "your uncle and aunt are filthy rich, aren't they, Wildman? This house has so many rooms they could have hidden you in one of them and nobody would have ever found you. Instead, they went into all the trouble of carrying you out of town and into the hills. Your Fae-blood must have really upset them."

"Which means they may be in league with the Temple or the military," I whisper. "This is a very bad idea. Kia... let's not do this. Let's just get out of town. We will be fine."

"We need food." Kiaran is chewing on the inside of his cheek, rubbing his fingers over his mouth, his blue eyes intent on the house. "And horses."

"Kia—"

"They owe." He nods. "Owe me. At least this."

"But—"

"We're going," Kiaran says, "to bring Finn back. Together."

A weight lifts off my chest. "Good, but Kia—"

He opens the gate of the house and strides inside. "Come on."

"You heard the man." Taj is grinning. "Come on."

Shaking my head, smiling in spite of everything, I let Taj haul me behind him, his hand wrapped around mine. Hope is flaring in my chest. If Kiaran is with us, part of our clan, my mate, and if he plans on helping us get Finnen back... Then hells yeah, I'll do whatever it takes.

For my mates, I'll do anything, everything, and it's not just my body demanding it anymore, it's my mind and my heart.

If fate is inevitable, so is love, too.

17

ARIADNE

Kiaran strides straight for the front door and we follow. I'm dazed from all that happened, stumbling after Taj.

Kiaran doesn't hesitate. He seems much more clear-headed than the rest of us. Frontal assault is the way to go, I suppose. After all, his family can't be expecting him to be alive, much less show up on their doorstep after all this time.

If they are still alive.

There's that to consider.

He slams the knocker on the door hard enough to break, and after a couple more of these thwacks, a harried-looking manservant opens the door.

"Yes?" He casts us a suspicious look and starts closing the door again. "I'm sorry, my masters have already donated to the Temple and we don't accept—"

"I'm Kiaran," Kiaran booms, shoving the door back into the startled servant's face. "Let me in."

The servant looks confused. "Apologies, who?"

"I want to speak to my aunt Eara and my uncle Faran,"

Kiaran says and strides into the house as if he owns it. "The D'Alerys."

It looks like sometimes lack of manners has its uses, because the servant is scrambling to go after him, but we push him aside as we enter, hot on Kiaran's heels, and find his family right there, in a side room.

Yeah, it seems fate has a sense of humor sometimes, because as it turns out, Kiaran's family are very much alive and kicking.

And very surprised to find him standing there, in front of them, hands balled at his sides, his tall frame filling the door.

"Who are you?" the man demands, standing up with some effort—more likely because of the many cushions on the sofa he has occupied than any infirmity, since his height rivals Kiaran's, and good gods, the family likeness is impossible to miss, although this man is much older, his beard white, and his face lined with creases of anger and annoyance. "What is the meaning of this intrusion?"

The room is richly appointed. Deep blue and green rugs on the floor and tapestries woven with scenes from the woods on the walls, velvet-covered sofas and low tables laden with trays and jars made of silver, embossed with figures and blossoms. Incense is burning in a corner and pastries and drink have been served, the aroma of butter and sugar almost eclipsing the scent of my mates.

"Your nephew." Kiaran bows his head, gaze blazing. "I am your nephew Kiaran."

"Such nonsense. We lost our nephew tragically in a fire many years ago. How dare you come and stir trouble here, in my house—"

"Husband," the woman says, rising and smoothing her long skirts. "Let me speak to him."

"You will do no such thing!" He thrusts an arm in front of her, his beard trembling with outrage. "He can't walk in here and make demands of us! We're honorable people. He's not our nephew."

"Husband," she tries again. "Please—"

"I don't care if you don't recognize me," Kiaran says slowly. "You help us. And you live."

The man's eyes widen. "You *threaten* us?"

"Of course I threaten you. I could kill you easily. But instead, I threaten you. You should thank me."

"You..."

"Faran," the woman says, grabbing the older man's hand. "Don't. He's our nephew."

"You can't possibly believe—!"

"Husband, you can't even lie to yourself. Kiaran survived. And the least we can do is help him."

He shakes her off, thunder on his face. "How dare you."

She sighs. Turns her gaze to Kiaran. "Take what you need. Just please, don't hurt us."

"Like you hurt me?" Kiaran demands, brows knit. "Are you sorry for it?"

His aunt glances at his uncle and turns her gaze away. "We did what we believed was right. We obey the Emperor's decrees. When your cousins' house burned down, we knew it was an omen. We had to do our duty."

Kiaran growls, taking a menacing step toward them, and I hurry to his side, taking his arm. "Kia, wait."

"Dammit," Taj mutters, grabbing his other arm. "They're not worth your time and energy, my man. Let them stew in their own misery and tea—though I'll take those cookies, they look good."

"Taj..." I roll my eyes to the heavens. "Come, Kia. Let's lock them in here and take what we need. We should be on our way by nightfall and time is running fast when you're busy."

———

"That was easy," I breathe as we secure the house, rounding up the servants and locking them up in another room, locking the doors and hoping nobody will show up at the door and get suspicious at the lack of reply. "Too easy."

"They weren't expecting anything like this to ever happen to them, is all." Taj is grinning from ear to ear, clearly in his element, twirling a knife in one hand. "Ambushing them like that... brilliant."

"They were terrified," I mutter.

"Damn right. The bastards deserve it."

"They do," I agree. Honestly, the more I think about it, the more I think that this is too light a punishment for wannabe murderers of children.

"Ah, here we go." Taj wrenches the cellar door open and a smell of mold and cold damp wafts up to us. "Where is Kiaran?"

"Good question."

"I'm going down to check what we can take with us. Find him and check the stables. If we can get three horses, we're set."

"Aye, sir." I try to smile but Finn's absence is grating on my nerves, my fears, my bones, my insides.

I gasp when Taj grabs my arms and hauls me in for a quick kiss. "We'll get him back, sweetheart. Like I said to him when we were looking for you, you have to have faith."

"Said by the man who's still doubting us."

"One of us has to keep a level head." He winks at me.

I say nothing to that because I still have my own doubts, and what right do I have to accuse my mates of the same affliction I suffer from?

"Look at me, *kora*." He brings a hand to my chin, tilting my head up so he can look into my eyes. His are bright and earnest. "Every day and night we spend together, our bond strengthens. The more I get to know all of you, the more I believe in us. And that's a lot to say for a military man without faith, one used to thinking in tactical advantages and maneuvers."

"Taj..."

"If this were a battle, sweets, I'd have called for immediate retreat long ago. In fact, I might have never engaged. The odds certainly aren't in our favor. The enemy has the upper hand. We're in danger and Finnen's abduction proved it."

"But—"

"But this is a war. Our war. Seeing the grand scale of it, I'm not stopping, not considering the danger. In a war, sometimes battles are lost on the way to victory."

"War? Grand scale? Are you talking about bringing the Fae back?"

"I'm talking about you and me and Kiaran and Finnen. About our family. That's the grand scale for me. As for the Fae, if our babies bring back the Lost Race, well, that's a different story."

The thought of babies always makes me shiver, excitement and fear warring in me.

The thought of being with my men makes me smile.

I want to laugh and weep and shove him away—or tear his clothes off him and climb him like a tree. "You're serious."

"Deadly. Now go before I ravish you right here and forget all about leaving this gods-forsaken town."

———

"We have to make sure that Finnen isn't still held here before we leave," I say, leaning against a table, watching Taj shave Kiaran. "That would be awful. I mean, what if they're still in town, looking for us?"

"That's only if they are certain he's one of us." Taj slides the blade over Kiaran's jaw, brows drawn together in concentration.

"Once they realized Finnen is blind, I doubt they'll connect him to us."

"Are you sure?"

"Sure? No. But the army is looking for me and two Temple people. They don't know Finnen is supposed to be blind, and besides, he's not dressed as a priest anymore. He saved us by running at them like that, distracting them as we hid. They didn't see us, or they'd have come after us. They probably thought they caught a madman and now are continuing on their way to the Summer Capital."

"Then we have to intercept them before they reach it," I say.

"Yeah, we must. We want to avoid the Lesser capital and its suburbs at all cost."

Taj has already shaved his bristly stubble, obviously not trusting Kiaran with the shaving blade, and he looks much younger now. Boyish, almost, with the dark hair curling at his temples. And as he shaves away Kiaran's beard, my Wildman's beauty shines through—the clean lines of his handsome face, his sharp cheekbones and chiseled jaw, his big blue eyes, his fine mouth. Each trait seems drawn in sharper lines than ever. Even his ears look more pointy.

"Well, if the army is expecting you to be with a man and a woman, won't they recognize us now as we attempt to leave the town?"

"Not if I am with two women," Taj says, leaning back to give Kiaran's now clean-shaved face a critical look.

"Two women?" Kiaran frowns at Taj. "What is this game?"

"A game of disguises. The guards won't look twice at a young aristocrat with his two sisters traveling to the capital for a matchmaking meeting."

"Taj..." I snort. "You wouldn't."

"He's pretty, isn't he?" Taj smirks at Kiaran. "Think he'll fool them?"

"What?" Kiaran glances from him to me and back, his frown turning into a scowl. "What are you saying?"

"Don't worry about it, Drakoryas." Taj pats Kiaran's shoulder. "I'll make you look good, trust me."

———

"This is a dress," Kiaran says, looking down at himself. "I want pants."

"Sorry, man, this is the only thing that would fit you." Taj's eyes sparkle. "Comfy, isn't it? And you can piss without any hassle. Just lift it. See?"

"Dresses are for women," Kiaran glowers at him. "I ask again, what is this game?"

"It's the best disguise," Taj says. "To get out of town. I'll bring pants for you to change into afterward, okay?"

"Not okay," Kiaran barks. "You wear dress, I wear pants!"

"Oh, dear Gods. You are prettier, okay? More Fae blood in you, by my guess. Come on, be a good sport."

I'm staring at Kiaran in the blue dress and can't deny that the fire raging in me flares at the sight. It's strange. Kiaran is as masculine as they come, no matter what Taj says, though sure, his face is a touch more delicate than Taj's. Could be his pale coloring, too.

But there's something so hot about the contrast between his hard jaw and broad shoulders and the corset, the long, flouncy skirt, the lace. Funny and sexy, too.

Making him look even more like a Wildman.

Even more like a man.

"We'll throw a shawl over his shoulders," Taj says, following my gaze. "And a hat on his head. It'll be fine."

"Are you sure you're not just doing this for your own perverse pleasure?" I arch a brow at him.

He shoots me a quick grin. "One has to suck every little pleasure out of life, sweetheart."

Kiaran is tugging at a lacy sleeve. "Itchy," he complains.

"We should hurry before Kiaran tears the dress off him," I say.

"Good thinking."

Then Kiaran grabs Taj and shoves him against the wall. "You," he hisses.

"Oops." Taj is still grinning like a fool. "Yes?"

"You make fun of me."

Taj's grin fades a little. "Listen, I'm serious. You look good, my man, and you'd be helping us."

"I don't look good." Kiaran glares.

"I don't want you any less in a dress, you idiot. I want you no matter what you wear, don't you get it? Just like I want Ariadne just as much in pants. You're a Wildman. Why are clothes important to you, huh?"

"Society," he mutters. "Finnen said... I must learn. Manners. Social norms."

"Fine, but we're not at a fancy social banquet. We're fleeing, and trust me, if I could pass for a pretty girl, I'd wear that dress in a heartbeat. I bet my ass will look great in that skirt."

With a harrumph, Kiaran gives him another shove in the chest and steps back. "You lie."

"I do not! You look great. It brings out your eyes." Taj grins wolfishly at Kiaran. "Right, Ari?"

"It does," I say firmly. "Shall we then?" I pat my own dress— we found plenty folded up carefully inside trunks in Kiaran's aunt's room, and mine is a cream-colored one, embroidered with dandelions, that flows over me like silk.

Come to think of it, it probably *is* silk.

Has to cost a fortune.

On top, I've pulled a long red woolen cloak with a hood. We

all chose cloaks with big hoods to cover our hair and faces as much as possible.

We're mostly set. Taj and Kiaran have already saddled three horses and filled their saddlebags with food and wine, water flasks hanging on either side, blankets rolled and tied behind each saddle.

"Let's go," Kiaran says and turns around to go. If anyone sees him swaggering past, they'll know for sure he's a man, and I hide a smile.

Taj sweeps on his cloak and nods. "Ready when you are."

"Let's go get our mate back," I whisper.

18

KIARAN

The more time I spend among people, the more memories return. Memories, knowledge, words, information I'd buried deep because in the wilderness it was useless, needless. Painful.

Being in this house, my uncle and aunt's house, has stirred up quite a few... remembrances.

Yeah, the words are coming back—slow and skulking like thieves in the night, often catching me unawares as they pop into my mind and it takes me some time to recognize them, place them.

I wasn't always a savage, it seems.

And even though spending... ten, twelve years on my own in the wilderness has made me who I am, it seems there is a deeper layer to me, the crust on top flaking away as I interact with other humans.

Or Fae. Whatever it is they are.

We are.

I remember the fire. The black smoke, suffocating, poisoning when I tried to approach. I had been outside, playing... with a kitten.

A ginger kitten.

Funny how that memory is so persistent, when the moment my aunt and uncle drove me to the countryside in their carriage and left me isn't there.

Too painful, I think. Too jagged and sharp to keep and touch.

Gone from my mind.

Though I do remember the carriage driving away as I stood under a tree, watching them go.

That memory stayed.

I put rocks under that tree. To mark it, somehow. I have often stood there, looking down at the valley, as if someone would return for me.

Nobody ever did.

I blame the crowding memories, all jumbled up and fucked up, for wandering the house like a ghost, not able to do much but stare at familiar objects and try to control my sadness and fury, trying not to open the door and punch my uncle in the face, force my aunt to her knees.

Demand their apology.

Demand their repentance.

And now, dressed in a ridiculous dress Taj put on me while I was lost in thought, I'm preparing to get on a horse, another activity I'm starting to remember from my childhood. I'd been trained to ride horses, as it turns out. And to write letters, though those still elude me.

I had friends.

And my cousins were mostly good to me.

What about my parents, though? A black hole in my memories. A missing page. How the fuck can I not remember them?

The most jagged piece of them all.

And damn, I hate this dress. How do girls move in these things? I stride toward the stables across the paved yard and the corset—that's what Ariadne called it, a corset—is digging in many unfortunate parts of me, while the wide skirt feels like I'm wearing a cloud, or a tree's foliage, my legs strangely bare. If I wasn't wearing my underpants underneath, which I did by threatening to bust Taj's balls if he as much as said another word on the matter, my dick would be swinging free.

Which is something I'm used to, after all this time.

But I've never spent my days and nights constantly fucking hard over a girl—and men—so that changes a lot of things.

Taj is talking with Ariadne, following behind me, their voices soothing, a melody like that of the rustling of leaves and the soughing of wind around my cave. My cave which I have left behind with everything I owned over the past twelve years, everything I found and fashioned and broke and mended, my entire life with the jaguars roaring outside and the hawks and vultures flying in circles overhead, the steep hills around me and the mountains in the distance, capped with snow.

I have made up my mind.

And the cave was just a cave, a place where I almost died of fucking loneliness and these people... my mates... they are where I belong.

I feel it in my gut, the way I feel danger when an animal is lurking in wait, the way I feel the rain coming down from the mountains.

This is my place. These are my people. This affection they show me is reflected in me. This desire they have for me is met in me.

"*Repeat the passage, Kiaran,*" a voice from my past says, a cane tapping on marble floors. "*What did philosopher Adrie say?*"

'*What I give is reflected in others and returns to me.*'

'*What others do to me is reflected in my heart and returned to them.*'

"What...?" I'm barely aware I've stopped and grabbed my

head. A painful throb goes through my skull, and another. "What the hell...?"

"Kiaran?" Ariadne's voice is distant, much more distant than the voices in my head. "What's wrong?"

I shake my head—which proves a mistake, as the pain grows worse—and then something whizzes past, leaving a burning line on my shoulder.

A knife thuds into the wooden door of the stables.

Fuck.

"Kiaran!" Taj roars, again making me think of jaguars, and I turn, grabbing Ariadne and pushing her behind me.

Where is the knife thrower? Judging from where the knife ended... I locate him behind a tree.

"Taj! Get him!" I point at the man and Taj is already moving, pulling out his knives and throwing them. He runs after them, right at the man, grabbing him and pulling him out of his hiding place.

A servant of the house that we missed in our search earlier.

"Trying to kill my mates, are you?" Taj snarls at the man and it takes me a long fucking moment to remember he's talking about us, that I'm one of those mates he's so fiercely protective of. "Thought you'd get a fat reward? That you'd get gratefulness? Are you that stupid?"

"Taj!" Ariadne is trying to step around me but I stop her. "We should get going, and Taj has gone..."

"... berserk?" I ask with a smirk.

She huffs. Not amused. "I was going to say rogue. Taj! Don't kill him!"

"Why not? He tried to kill Kiaran," Taj replies, his fist bunched up in the front of the man's shirt, shaking him. "Why should I show clemency?"

He'd kill him for *me*?

"Because Kiaran is alive," Ariadne says, "we're all alive and we have to go get Finnen!"

"Taj," I say, "leave him be. Ariadne is right. He's just a servant."

Why should I care about killing him when I've allowed my aunt and uncle to live?

Maybe Taj hears some of what I'm thinking in my voice, because he lets go of the man and shoves him to the ground. Then he stalks back to us, face like a thundercloud, fists clenched.

First he grabs Ariadne, pats her shoulders, her waist.

"I'm fine," she whispers, obviously understanding what he won't ask. "I'm unharmed."

Then he turns to me. "Show me where he hurt you," he growls.

I frown right back. "It's nothing."

With another growl, he pulls the sleeve off my shoulder—it's mostly off anyway, as if my shoulders would ever fit in a delicate dress—and leans in to inspect the wound.

"You'll live," he says.

"Yeah."

"Don't let anyone throw knives at you again."

"Are arrows okay?" I grumble. "Just to be clear."

His mouth twitches. "Are you and Finnen twins separated at birth or what? Hear that, Ari? Our Wildman seems to have a sense of humor after all." He turns his gray gaze on me. "No arrows. Not even in jest. You're ours. I'll kill whoever dares hurt you."

I can only nod, still kind of dazed. We protect our omega, that goes without saying, but I never thought...

Fuck, I never thought I might be considered important in the group as well. Important enough to kill for.

I'm still examining the feeling when Taj leads the way into the stables and our saddled horses. At least I'm too distracted to be pissed at him for dressing me up in this frothy thing that's already coming apart at the seams. My aunt has never been a slim woman but I bet she never imagined a man of my size would be wearing her dresses.

My mouth twitches, for some reason.

And then I'm furious again, and sad, so fucking sad I think my heart is breaking. My chest aches with remembered agony and fear.

You're not that child anymore, I remind myself. *And you're not alone anymore. Stop thinking and get moving.*

Fucking move.

Taj is giving Ariadne a leg up onto the saddle. I turn to look at my horse and he returns my gaze. This horse looks annoyed.

Comparing dicks with a horse won't come out in my favor. I bare my teeth at the stallion and hope he'll let me ride him.

To be fair, in his place, I wouldn't be happy with this arrangement, either.

"Hi, horse." I grab the bridle, swinging myself up onto the saddle. Even remembering parts of my childhood and the fact I had riding lessons don't mean I'm an experienced rider. At least I know how to sit in the saddle.

I think of my cave, the hills, the birds, the jaguars, wolves and wild boars.

I think of freedom.

Then I glance at Ariadne astride her mare and Taj getting on another stallion, and I find myself grinning.

Freedom is overrated, I think and pat my horse's neck, then snatch my hand back when he turns and tries to bite me. *Freedom isn't everything. Affection, a human touch, desire, ease, spending time with people you like, people you care for...*

That's everything.

Though a slave may not think that way. Once I have committed myself to this bond, is there a way out?

And do I want one?

———

We walk our horses out of the gate and onto the street. A woman sweeping her porch stares at us. Another grabs a little boy playing with a wooden ball and moves him out of the way of the horses' hooves. The day is drab but dry, clouds blanketing the sky. The town seems to melt into their gray shades, the earth fading into the sky.

We all have our hoods pulled low over our faces and let Taj lead.

He'll pay for this, I think, glaring at the back of his head, and an image pops in my head of Taj lying on a bed, legs spread, his cock hard and leaking, his hands tied over his head.

Oh yeah. He'll pay for this.

As we amble through the town, keeping a slow pace not to make anyone suspicious, I spend some time thinking of ways to make Taj pay, tied up and spread for me, Ariadne helping me mete out punishment.

Another reason freedom is overrated. Jacking off to imaginary people is a lot less satisfying than actual sex.

I remember taking Ariadne in the bathtub, I remember her getting fucked by Taj, perfectly recall her straddling Finnen on the bed and the noises she made as he fingerfucked her.

Oh yeah, I'm ready to be '*civilized.*'

Finnen's voice echoes in my head and I grit my teeth. We need him back. Ariadne needs him. We need him, that grumpy bastard of a priest. Ariadne's the glue holding us together but he's a nail on which we turn and spin.

Part of a whole, I think. *We're parts of a whole. We're—*

"Watch out!" Ariadne shouts and I pull the reins on my bitey stallion just in time. Though of course my horse wouldn't just crash into Ariadne's—but he's dancing right and left, snorting and tossing his head.

'If you don't control your horse,' a voice says in my head, *'it will control you. Always be in control, Kiaran.'*

"What?" I blink, shake my head to dislodge the

disembodied voice that goes on talking about the reins and the stirrups and the saddle and the position of the rider.

"Kia!"

We've reached the main street and a crowd of people is blocking us. Behind them, I see tall colorful hats and banners passing with the symbol of the tree reaching to the heavens, a dragon coiled in its branches.

A Temple procession.

Fuck.

"Turn back!" Taj yells at us. "Turn around. We find another way."

So I wheel my horse about, and he resists my tugging on the reins, eyes wild and tread uneven. "Come on, horse. Move your ass."

Maybe he doesn't like crowds.

"I don't like crowds, either," I tell him, leaning over his mane as he finally does my bidding and turns around, "but we don't always get a choice, do we?"

He whinnies and snorts and gnaws on the bit, hooves dancing on the cobblestones. I'm a bad rider, can't control him as I should, but nothing to do about it now.

I lead our little group through the streets, hopelessly fucking lost in this town where every corner seems to wake up a memory and yet nothing tells me which way to go. I was a child, didn't have a clear map of the town in my head when I was carried away and left to die in the wild. No amount of childhood memories will tell me where the southern gate is...

... but I close my eyes for a moment, and I know, I *know* which way is south. I feel the north pulling at me, I feel the south pushing.

"I felt it," I breathe, pulling on the reins. "I felt the south."

"What are you talking about?" Taj snaps, riding to my side.

"I feel the south." I point. "That way. We're going wrong."

"Damn. Just like Finnen said."

"We're going the wrong way?" Ariadne pulls up her horse on my other side. She fans herself with her hand and her cheeks are flushed under the hood. "Goddess, I'm burning. It's too warm."

I blink at her. "Warm?" I'm frozen solid, can't feel my nose or hands, and the wind blowing from the west has blades in it.

"The more time we spend with our omega," Taj says, "the hotter she will become. Quite literally."

I snort.

"Not funny," Ariadne mutters.

"And the more Fae traits will appear," Taj goes on. "In all of us. Those traits we have will become more apparent."

"You mean, we'll turn into full Fae?" Ariadne sounds slightly appalled. "Big pointy ears and sharp teeth?"

I don't know how the hell I feel about that. Besides, my teeth are already sharp. "Sensing the south is a Fae trait?

"Finnen talked about it. Said I should be able to feel it too if I tried," Taj says. "He implied I wasn't making enough of an effort."

I chuckle, dig my heels in and turn my resisting horse toward the south. "That sounds like Finnen."

"Wait," Taj calls out as I take the lead. "I should be at the front."

"Should you, now." I smirk. He thinks a dress will make me hang back? As if a dress ever stopped Ariadne from doing whatever the hell she wanted.

As if a dress makes a woman. As if a woman can't do the things a man can.

As if social norms mean anything at all. They're the reason we were all cast away in the first place.

And I'm a berserk Drakoryas Wildman. Does Taj really think I'll sit and fetch like a good dog? I'm insane by definition.

It's my strength.

And as I canter down one street, then another, I come upon a military patrol.

"Back!" Taj shouts. "Turn back!"

"Kia!" Ariadne is wheeling her horse around already. "Come on."

"We were going to ask them a question." I press forward and hear them both cursing behind me.

"Kia, not now!"

"Then when?" I growl and don't stop. My stallion leaps forward and we reach the end of the street in the blink of an eye. "No better time than now."

The patrol stops, the soldiers staring at me. I must present quite the picture—a muscular, broad-shouldered lady in a frilly dress astride a black crazed-eyed stallion who can't keep still.

"Who goes there?" one of them asks, then more cautiously, "My lady?"

Controlling my horse is taking up a lot of my attention, but I manage to stay in front of them as Ariadne and Taj return behind me. "The soldiers passing through the town this morning, where did they head to?"

A ripple goes through the patrol.

"Good day, brave men at arms." Ariadne nudges her horse beside mine. "We are looking for my brother, a soldier in the army, to give him news of our mother's passing. We were told he'd be heading to the Summer Capital, crossing through here, but his brigade may have left town already."

"Are you referring to the Firebrand Brigade, my lady?" another soldier says. "That's one of the elite troops and they indeed passed through here earlier today, heading to the capital. We've heard rumors they are hunting after some renegade military Fae-bloods. I'm sorry to hear about your mother's passing."

"Thank you, kind sir." Ariadne looks away and I don't think her sorrow is feigned. "I appreciate it."

"So they have already left the town?" Taj asks. "Are you sure?"

"Yes, my lord." The soldiers exchange glances. "They must be near the town of Tajen by now."

"Thank you for your help," Ariadne says.

"We'll catch up." I nudge the stallion around. "Come on, horse."

"My beautiful lady," the soldier says and steps toward me. "You're bleeding. Your shoulder. Let me take a look. You shouldn't be riding like that, we can help—"

"Fuck off," I snarl and jab my heels into the horse's sides. "Let's go!"

Leaving some very confused soldiers behind, we turn south.

19

ARIADNE

Kiaran wheels his huge horse about and starts down another street, strangely sexy and incongruous in that blue dress and the green cape on top, pale locks escaping the hood.

The soldier is still looking forlornly after him, and I almost laugh.

Poor soldier, falling for the blue-clad, blue-eyed lady who is in reality a muscular Wildman in disguise.

I turn my mare around and follow him, trusting him to lead us in the right direction. A girl on the street catches my eye as I nudge my horse to a faster walk, a blond girl who reminds me of Ismere.

My friend at the Fort Temple, who turned against me so easily.

I wonder what happened to her. I remember her, standing beside high priest Elegos as my fate played out, as I was accused and condemned. At the expression on her face.

It had looked like satisfaction, I think, but was it, really? Did I really not know her mind at all?

It's hard to accept you've been so wrong, for so long.

But what if I'm imagining that look of pleasure on her face? What if she was, in fact, afraid? Panicked? My own perception was colored by shock and fear.

We canter through the streets, avoiding the procession, making for the southern gate of the town. Time is of the essence if we want to catch up with the Brigade, though how we're meant to tackle them and rescue Finnen is another story. I hope Taj has a plan.

First of all, we need to get out of this town before anyone gets suspicious and stops us. I'm starting to think that Taj's strategy of dressing Kiaran up is either genius or the mother of all bad ideas. I mean, that soldier was perhaps smitten—but Kiaran still looks like a Wildman in a dress. An alpha in an omega's usual attire.

People are bound to take notice.

At least, he's leading us through the streets at a fast pace, obviously sure of the direction. Can I feel the cardinal directions, too, or is it only an alpha thing?

Not something to try as you're riding through a hostile town, but maybe later... I want to ask Taj more, later, about his claim that more Fae traits will appear as our bond strengthens.

I want to know all he knows, what to expect and what to prepare for.

My belly cramps and I bow over my mare's back. *Ow.* At least it's not as bad as it was a few days ago. Our night at the inn seems to have helped—though now I feel like I'm burning from the inside.

My heat is coming on.

Not now, I pray to whomever God or Goddess might be listening. *I need to get Finnen back first, please. Not now...*

The houses flit by, trees and iron-wrought gates, mules and carts and horses and people. My hood falls back and I grab it, pull it back over my face. Not that it matters. Nobody knows me. The whole point is to not get stopped, not get interrogated.

That nobody notices the pointed ears Kiaran hides under his hood, or the scale pattern on Taj's back.

No Fae traits for me, not yet, or maybe not ever? Strangely, I feel bereft, needing that connection to my mates.

Sometimes it only happens if you are with child, Taj had said. I definitely need to ask him more questions about it.

Later.

At last, I make out the town walls and the gate from afar. A small crowd mills about it, and my heart sinks.

The guards are controlling the in and out. Usually, they just nod and go back to dozing, like they did when we entered, but the Temple or the army must have alerted them to take note of who enters and leaves.

"Keep your hoods down," I hiss, "and Taj, take the lead!"

Kiaran barely slows down, but Taj digs his heels in and snaps the reins, overtaking him, shooting him a glare.

Men. Alphas. It doesn't matter if you're raised with wolves and jaguars, in the army or the Temple, it seems. They won't stop competing, no matter what.

How did I end up with a bunch of alphas? They are as alien to me as the jaguars and wolves of the wild.

Alien but also so dear, and I grin when Kiaran rallies his restless stallion to walk almost side by side with Taj as they reach the gate.

And then he turns and smirks at me, as if to say, *"see? I did it,"* and I laugh outright.

Such boys.

Smothering another laugh, I join the line at the gate. With luck, we'll pass inspection without trouble. In this, Taj was right. Changing the picture with two women and one man should throw them off our scent.

The gates loom over us, closer and closer. A little girl, gripping tightly her mother's hand, is pointing at us with a chubby finger. Her mother is staring.

But Kiaran's hood is pulled low, as is mine, and the guards cast us a fairly uninterested look as we approach their posts on either side of the gate.

It looks like we'll just walk right through, and a nervous giggle almost escapes me as the other guard waves us on, pushing his helmet back to scratch at his brow.

Almost, almost there...

"Halt!" someone shouts, "halt them! In the name of Holy Barazyos, stop!"

Taj's horse rears back when the guards cross their spears in front of him, and Kiaran's stallion whinnies and dances right and left.

"What's the meaning of this?" Taj demands, his voice carrying over everyone, every inch the affronted, arrogant rich lord. "How dare you stop us?"

"My lord," one of the guards says, "who are you and who are your companions?"

"The nerve," Taj says, all haughty and disdainful, and I'd grin if I wasn't panicking inside. "We are of the House of Draigos, heading to Eremis to visit family. Only passing through here, so I'd thank you to step aside and let us leave."

By now, the man shouting for us to halt has reached us, panting and red-faced. "The house of the D'Alerys was robbed," he wheezes, pointing at Kiaran, "and a witness says one of the men was dressed as a woman. It has to be you."

Oh, dear goddess. Lights flash over my mates as a strange fury grips me. I reach for the knife I have sheathed at my belt, stolen from the D'Alerys' vast cellar. Finnen told me that the rituals I've practiced all my life are fighting techniques, and the ritual of the Swirling Heron comes to my mind, danced with two blades. I have one, and it will have to do.

One blade is enough to take a man down.

"You imply that we are robbers and thieves?" Taj roars. "You insult our House! The gods will punish you after I'm done with you."

"Taj," I whisper. More guards are gathering, drawing swords or raising spears. We are vastly outnumbered. No ritual of Artume has prepared me for an actual battle. "We have to retreat..."

"It's just me and my sisters," Taj goes on. "Let us through. Or are you implying that one of my sisters is a man?"

"She is rather masculine," one of the guards says quietly.

"And so what? Should I love her any less? Does that make her any less of a woman?"

The guards look confused, exchanging glances between them.

Kiaran growls, and turns his horse to the side, facing the guards. Then he charges them, his stallion whinnying.

"Oh no! Kia!"

"Here comes a Drakoryas!" he roars, and the guards scatter like a flock of sparrows when a hawk dives down.

"Berserk!" people scream, starting to run and I wonder what they see. "Berserk!"

"Ari! Come on!" Taj gestures and, tightening my hold on the reins, leaning over the horse's neck, I nudge my horse forward.

"Yah!" I cross the gate on the heels of Taj's horse, and look over my shoulder at the mess now behind us. Guards are running in every direction, some of them screaming, townsfolk shouting and climbing over one another to get away from the rider in their center, cries of "Drakoryas" echoing.

And Kiaran...

He's charging this way and that, his hood fallen back, the corset of the dress torn and hanging off his powerful chest, a snarl on his face and a glow about him.

There's a wild energy surrounding him, crackling in the air, a whirlwind of darkness and light, flashes on his chest and arms. His bellow is that of a mad bull, of thunder, of a god himself.

I catch myself staring, my horse slowing down, coming to a stop. Taj is staring, too.

"Holy shit," he whispers. "I heard stories of the Drakoryas in battle. I never thought I'd see one in action."

"Is that normal? It feels like... like magic."

"I wouldn't know," Taj says, his voice hushed, "but I'd say that the blackness writhing about him and the flashes of light aren't quite what you'd expect from a human."

"We're changing," I whisper. "Is this why the Council is so scared of us?"

"You mean they're not just bigots and prudes?" Taj winks at me.

I shake my head.

"We should get going," Taj says. "Kiaran!"

"Kiaran!" I yell, whirling my horse about. "Kiaran, to us! Come to us!"

At first, I think he can't hear us and I prepare to ride back to him, grab the reins of his horse and pull him after us, if that strange whirlwind doesn't suck me in, and I see Taj preparing to do the same—but then Kiaran wheels his horse around toward us.

His pale locks seem to have unwound, each strand standing up, a bright silver halo around his face, and his eyes look like black pits, lips peeled back, gums dark, teeth yellow and sharp, his ears long and sharply pointed.

"What...?" I pull on the reins and my mare neighs and shakes. "Kia?"

He charges toward us, and Taj swears.

"Back!" He tries to grab the reins from me, but I don't let him. "Run, Ari!"

"He won't hurt us," I whisper, frozen, watching him race toward us. It's as if time has slowed down to a trickle, and every leap his horse takes lasts a lifetime. It's like watching death ride toward you.

Is he aware of his surroundings? Does the legendary craze that grips the berserks have a hold on him now? Will he mow us down as he's been doing with the guards, unable to separate friend from foe?

"Kia!" I breathe. He's charging right at us, right at me—

"Ride!" he shouts, riding right past us, one hand held high. "Ride now!"

I'm still staring at the afterimage of him, bare-chested, the blue, frilly skirt over his legs and saddle, his pale hair wild, galloping at me, and I blink dazedly, my body clenching with arousal and need. What I want...

What I want is to pull him off that horse and push him down in the grass and churned earth, straddle him, press my mouth to him, then tear that skirt off him and put my mouth on his cock, suck and bathed it with my tongue until he comes, until the whirlwind dies and something new is born.

Then Taj whoops, breaking through the loop of lusty thoughts. "Let's go! To the south!"

"Yes, let's go," I whisper, shaking my head to clear it, curling an arm around my aching middle. Casting the gray town with its Temple banner and Kiaran's awful family one last glance, I turn my horse to the south. "Let's find our Finnen."

20

ARIADNE

"Hey." Kiaran has finally slowed down and I dig my heels into my horse's sides, urging it to go faster until I'm riding beside my Wildman. "Everything okay?"

Kiaran shoots me a quick look, then at Taj who is riding a few paces away, his face revealing nothing. He looks perfectly normal once more. Well, apart from the remnants of the blue dress still clinging to his body. Perfectly human.

Makes me wonder whether I imagined things.

"I bet they've never seen anyone like you in these parts," I say, trying for light. "They'll weave stories about you, tell their grandchildren about the day a Drakoryas chased the guards away from their town gate."

He's still silent. Our horses are walking slowly. Soon we'll have to make camp, let them graze and rest.

He worries me. He hasn't spoken a word since he galloped out of the town and told us to ride.

"That was brave," I try again. "You gave us a chance to ride away. Faced them all on your own. That was impressive, and you—"

"I went berserk."

Those three quiet words are harsh and jagged.

"You saved our lives. Allowed us to leave the town." Something in his expression makes me ask, "Has it happened before?"

"No."

"Ah." Now I understand his silence. "But you—"

"I wanted to kill them. Crush their skulls in my hand. See their blood flow."

"Right. About that—"

"You were angry," Taj says, riding closer to us. "Weren't you?"

Kiaran glances at him, nods.

"Why?"

"I have to protect you."

"This isn't the usual bloodlust," Taj says. "This is your alpha's protective instinct toward your omega and alpha mates kicking in."

"You know everything, huh?" Kiaran scowls at him, then looks down at his hands on the pommel of the saddle.

"I know enough. To induce the battle craze, they give Drakoryas mead and powder of *echevon*. Just because you grew up like a wild animal doesn't mean you're any different physiologically from any other man, Kia. But being an alpha sharing a bond with an omega and other alphas, that... that changes you. It's not just you. Any one of us could have gotten the bloodlust. Only you are more... open to your emotions."

"What the hell do you mean?" Kiaran snarls.

"You are readier than the rest of us to enter this bond. You may not be always able to name your emotions, but you don't fight them because your family, your society or your superiors told you so, like we do. You have this advantage over us."

"Emotions... are no advantage," he mutters and still looks

troubled. "And you don't really know... how I feel. You talk and talk, but have no idea."

"Whatever," Taj mutters, frowning.

Kiaran may be right. Or Taj. I don't know.

"All I know is..." I lean to the side, brush my hand over his arm. "I'm grateful you are with us, Kiaran."

He gives a slight nod, and I think his expression lightens, so I'll take that as a good sign.

Nobody wants to act like a madman. Nobody wants to lose control.

But it seems that this bond between us, this thing building between the four of us, is all about giving up control and letting nature take its course.

———

The problem with letting nature take its course, of course, is spending a day in pure misery on the saddle, my blood boiling in my veins and my belly cramping again and again. It makes me antsy and cagey, angry at the world. Constant pain and discomfort can do that to you, and my worry about Finnen isn't helping.

Is he all right? Has he managed to keep his smartass mouth shut or did he egg on the soldiers until they beat the smarts out of him?

We canter past more towns on top of hills, some of them spilling down to the riverside. We have finally reached the river Ekelon, into which most streams pour sooner or later to form the great waterway leading to the summer capital and from there to the sea.

Taj talks about that when we slow down to a walk in the afternoon—about the barges he's seen during campaigns heading south, laden with barrels of mead and boxes of silk cloth and iron, about the noisy ports on the river as the country gives way from rock and forest to steppe and urban centers.

He says he's come close to the border with the Rising Moon Lands but has never crossed over.

His voice is starting to sound distant, the voice of a storyteller sitting by a fire, and the fire is burning me, licking at my skin, at my breasts and neck, flowing down, between my legs. I'm so hot, too hot, and my eyes are misting over, black seeping into my vision.

"Barges?" Kiaran asks.

"Long, flat river boats," Taj says." The river flows through the capital and there is a great port there, called the—"

"—Tulfa," Kiaran says, "for the old Temple there."

"Funny you should know that," Taj says, sounding thoughtful. "Memories returning?"

"Some," Kiaran says.

"An old Temple, yeah, where gods and goddesses were worshipped by the Fae, now used as a market hall. Some say those gods will curse us and bring about our downfall for using their sacred hall in such a way."

"Fools," Kiaran mutters.

"You don't think the gods might curse us?"

"They already have."

Taj chuckles.

But it's true, isn't it? I think. *We're cursed—to carry the Fae blood and not to know what to do with it, how to deal with these instincts, these urges that humans barely experience.*

I'm cursed—or blessed? It sure feels like a curse right now, with the pain and burning in my body, and...

"Ari!" Taj barks. "What's wrong?"

"Hot," I whisper, blinking black spots from my eyes. "Burns..."

"It's her heat coming on," Taj is saying, his voice growing distant again.

"She's in heat?" Kiaran asks.

"Not fully yet. I heard omegas can go crazy with it if they don't have their alphas to get them through it, but she's definitely getting closer."

"Don't talk about me... as if I'm not here," I rasp, clenching my hands on the pommel of the saddle. The world tilts. "I can hear you."

"Great, then listen good: We're making camp now and taking care of you, girl. Just hold on tight for a few more moments until we find a good place to stop."

His voice comes in echoes. I slump over the saddle, nausea turning my stomach, and hope to survive what my body needs.

———

"Ari." Kiaran's face swims into view sometime later. He's pulling me down from the saddle and I let him. He gathers me in his arms, swings me up against his chest, his face a pale shape over me, his eyes bright like candles. "You'll be okay."

I rest my head on his shoulder and draw in his scent, my body instantly tightening, my core clenching. I'm already getting wet between my legs, and I ache.

How I ache for him.

I whine low in my throat, running my hand over his bare chest. His hair, untangled and loose now, tickles my face, and it smells of him—of pine and resin and spice.

"Here," Taj says and my gaze swings to him. He's leading the three horses toward a cluster of cypresses, tall and dark like black flames, interspersed with proud oaks. "We'll camp here."

My gaze follows his tall form, his broad back, his tight ass inside his black pants, his dark, tousled head, and a moan escapes me.

I want.

I want him. I want them both so badly I think I'm dying. I'll die if I don't get between them, naked, skin on skin, to touch and taste and feel.

And be taken.

Goddess, my legs tremble, my thighs clench at the thought.

Kiaran who is striding after Taj and the horses makes a shushing, soothing noise at me. It's more of a purr, I think, rumbling through his chest, through me, and some of the pain fades.

Sighing, I close my eyes, trusting him, trusting both of them to help me.

I've never felt so needy, so helpless, so dependent on anyone in my life and it scares the crap out of me—but this is the whole point, isn't it? That I need these men, that I chose them to be my family, to help me through this heat, and in return...

In return, I'll give them cute babies.

Sweet goddess... Not the role I'd ever seen myself in, but thinking of babies, chubby cheeks and small chubby feet, is starting to feel more and more natural. More and more... lovely. They'd have Taj's gray eyes, or Kiaran's blue ones, or Finnen's... Yet again I wonder if he was born blind or if something happened to take away his sight. I've never asked him, have I? So much to talk about with them, so much to uncover—

"Here, put her down here," Taj says, interrupting my wandering thoughts. "Gently."

"I am gentle," Kiaran snaps and lowers me on top of soft fabric.

It's Taj's cloak, I realize belatedly, spread on a patch of soft grass under the vast umbrella of an oak's branches and foliage. Kiaran kneels down beside me, looking like a forest god with his sculpted body and the remnants of the blue silk over his legs.

There's a big tent in the silk.

He's hard.

And just like that, the heat returns, and I reach for him. "Kia..."

He falls on me like a man famished, his lips colliding with mine, his tall body shoving me onto my back, lying heavy on top of me as he ravishes my mouth. It's clumsy like the last time, brutal, his teeth clacking against mine, his teeth biting into my lips, his hard cock rubbing between my legs even as I spread them, welcoming him.

My hands wind around his neck, sliding on blood, though he barely flinches when I touch the wound on his shoulder. I'm so lost in the haze of arousal I barely notice, too, not enough headspace left to worry about hurting him, about having to bind that wound.

I need him naked, I need my own undergarments off so I can really feel him, so I can guide him inside me, or just offer myself to him, let him take what he wants.

After all, I want the same.

His mouth is glued to mine, his lips moving over my lips, sending jolts of arousal through me. He wrestles with my corset but can't seem to be able to pull it down.

"Kia, let me. Kiaran!" Taj is there, kneeling beside us, a familiar tent in his dark pants, his eyes blazing. "Don't tear her dress, we don't have another. Move!"

I clutch at Kiaran's shoulders, to keep him there, even as he pulls his mouth from mine. "No!"

"I'll undress you," Taj growls, "and then we'll pleasure you as you deserve, kitten."

"Mine," Kiaran growls right back, baring his teeth at Taj. "Fuck off."

"Ours," Taj says, and something in Kiaran eases. "Our omega, our mate, and we'll pleasure her. Together."

"But—" I begin.

"When she goes into heat, we'll take her hard and fast, over and over," Taj says, shoving Kiaran off me. "But now... now we get a chance to make her see stars, my friend. Don't you want to know how?"

"Fuck." Kiaran finally rolls off me. "Pleasure her. I want that."

"Taj," I whine. "What are you doing? I want you inside me. Both of you. I don't care about games."

"This isn't a game, love," he whispers, leaning over me. "This is about making you feel so good you'll forget your own name, trust me on this. Don't knock it until you've tried it."

"Tried what?" Kiaran has a scowl on his face. He grabs his cock through the blue silk, groans. "I want to fuck her."

Me, too, but when I open my mouth to say so, Taj bends his head and takes my mouth. He slants his mouth, slides his lips over mine once, twice, then his tongue slips into my mouth, stroking and licking and thrusting, while his lips still move, caressing, stoking the fire in my core until I clench so hard I almost come.

He breaks the kiss and I chase after him, panting.

Oh, holy shit...

"Like that." Taj wears a satisfied look on his handsome face. "Pleasuring her, turning every touch into more."

"She liked it," Kiaran says, his tone accusing and baffled at the same time. "Show me how."

"I will."

"Show me!"

"Come here." Taj grabs Kiaran who's still scowling, sliding his hand around Kiaran's head, and brings their mouths together. He kisses Kiaran and I prop myself up on my elbows to watch, breathless, as he does to him what I felt him doing to me—slanting his mouth, pressing it more firmly against Kiaran's as he explores it with his tongue, moving his lips over Kiaran's in slow motions.

Kiaran groans, grabbing Taj's shoulders, kissing him back, pressing his body to Taj's, and Gods above, I think I'm about to self-combust. Helplessly, I slip a hand under my skirt, between my legs where I'm hot and wet, and rub a little.

I gasp, arousal flaring even hotter.

"No." Taj has broken the kiss with Kiaran and is reaching for my hand. "You only come when I say so, my pretty."

"But I…"

"I know you need it. I know you want it. But I'm not done with you yet."

"I'm so close," I whisper. "And I want you inside me."

"I know." He strokes Kiaran's jaw, but his gaze is fixed now on me. "I made fun of Finnen for not knowing how to pleasure a woman, but I never pleasured you, only took my pleasure with you. Our first time together and I fucked you without taking my time to make it good for you."

"Do you regret it?" I ask. "It was good for me, you know."

"No regrets, but this time I will make you scream with pleasure. You, Wildman, watch and take notes."

"Notes." Kiaran looks dazed, his hand moving over his cock. He's finally torn off the silky skirt and undergarments he's gripping that rod of pale flesh in his fist, the purple head of his cock glistening wet with every stroke. "What notes…?"

Taj starts undoing the laces of my corset, his deft fingers moving quickly, pulling the laces from their eyelets, making quick work of them, and in no time, he's opening my corset, leaving me in my fine dress. Then he pulls the dress down, pulls on my sleeves until the top pools around my waist and I'm left in my chemise.

"Dammit," he snarls, "how many layers are there?" And he tugs my dress down and down until I'm free of it and I'm left dressed in my undergarments. "I liked it more when you wore pants and a shirt. Easier to get you naked."

Kiaran growls his agreement, his eyes glued on me, on every inch of my skin revealed by Taj's ministrations. "I'd just rip it off her."

"I know. Trust me, if I don't get her naked damn soon, I'll say fuck it and do just that," Taj mutters.

My chemise is loose and easier to pull off me. I let him manhandle me like a doll, turn me this way and that, pulling my clothes off, but once he drags my chemise and underpants off me, leaving me naked on his cloak, I grip his broad shoulders and pull him down on top of me.

Taj groans, dips his head to take one of my nipples between his teeth, and I gasp, arching back. He gently torments the small nub, sucking on it, worrying at it, sending shocks of pleasure through me.

"What are you doing?" Kiaran demands, scooting closer, until all I can see above me is his handsome face, flushed, eyes glittering. "She likes that?"

Taj flicks his tongue over my nipple, over and over, and I moan, shaking underneath him, my eyes closing.

Goddess...

By the time he finally releases the tortured nub, I'm dripping wet and rocking my hips, needing friction, anything to make the ache inside me stop.

"Try it." Taj gestures for Kiaran to come closer. "You know what feels good. You've been with her before. Do it."

With a bitten-off grunt, Kiaran bends over me, taking my other nipple in his mouth. His teeth bite a little harder, his lips suck with rough force, and I arch up with a cry.

"Please..."

Kiaran draws back. "Fucking, now."

Taj curses. "I had plans, dammit, but I need to be inside you, sweetheart." He fumbles with the laces at the front of his pants, pulling out his big, hard cock. "Are you ready?"

21

TAJ

uck. I honestly had planned to take my time with her this time, take it slow, explore every inch of her mouthwatering body, lick every inch of her silky skin, dip my tongue into every crevice and drag it over her nipples and her wet pussy... taste her everywhere, make her come over and over before I plunged my cock into her.

But she's so ready, so wet and hot, her moans setting me on fire, and Kiaran is already between her legs, pushing me over, his cock trembling against his belly.

I suppose lesson time is over.

It's time to fuck.

And I thought I was more civilized than our Wildman, but I find myself growling and grabbing his hips, trying to pull him away from our omega to claim her myself first.

Kiaran slams his hand into my side, where the wound he fucking gave me still isn't fully healed, and I gasp, hunching over.

"Taj," Ariadne reaches her hand out to me. I thought she wouldn't notice, but of course she does. "He hurt you."

Kiaran shoots a sideways glance at me, blue eyes dark and

blank with desire. He has his cock poised at her entrance, his muscular body shaking with barely-there control. He probably didn't realize what he did.

And he pushes into her, one long, hard thrust.

She cries out, head falling back, mouth open.

I should teach him not to do that, not without knowing she's ready, not without checking—but fuck, that's damn hot.

And from the way she's now panting and rocking her hips up to meet him, it looks like she was fucking ready.

As I am.

I watch avidly as the Wildman fucks her. His muscular ass clenches with each thrust, powerful thighs working as he pistons in and out of her, and I push down my pants to take my cock in hand. He has pulled one of her legs up, bending it at the knee, and is gazing down where he's plunging into her.

I want to touch him, too, press my cock against his back, rub it where it dimples with muscles.

Instead, I throw my arm over his shoulders and watch as he ruts. He growls a little at me, at the distraction, maybe even at the touch, though he's a pretty much touchy-feely kind of guy, unlike Finnen—but he's so focused on fucking her that he doesn't even falter in his rhythm.

I watch from my vantage point his cock pushing into her rosy folds, her slick smeared all over her inner thighs, as her small clit juts, hard and wet and flushed, as her breasts rock with his every thrust.

Fuck...

I'm working my cock as slowly as I can manage, afraid I'll come before I get my turn. Kiaran is panting, groaning. Then he pulls her leg, wrapping it around his thigh, and settles between her legs, lying almost on top of her.

I bite the inside of my cheek, my hand flying over my cock as he grunts and ruts into her, his pale hair falling in a curtain over his face, obscuring it, his pale shoulders bunching with muscles as he braces his hands on the cloak by her head to thrust harder, deeper.

They come almost at the same time, her wail of pleasure mingling with his deep groan. His rhythm falters and he thrusts one last time before he stills, small shudders shaking his frame as he spills inside her.

This time, when I grab and haul him off her, he rolls away, a grin on his face and his eyes closed. I press myself between her legs and she reaches for me, moaning my name.

"I'm here, my pretty," I breathe, "right here. Feel me."

She gasps when I push into her—dripping wet, hot and tight. Her pussy hugs my cock so perfectly I almost shoot my load. Looking down at her pale body, spread underneath me like an offering, makes me feel like a god. I try to take it slow—I try damn hard—but her pussy welcomes me, sucking my cock in, shattering reason.

It's... fucking impossible to hold back. The need only seems to increase with every thrust, arousal mounting in a colossal wave, about to wash me away. I fall over her, catching myself on my elbows and not feeling the impact. My mouth is a breath away from hers, her eyes glimmering under long lashes, and I kiss her.

A grunt escapes me as the mark on my back begins to burn, but it's lost in the maelstrom of sensations. Her nipples are hard points against my skin, her belly silky, her pussy velvety hot. We breathe in each other's moans as we rock together, kissing and kissing, pleasure feeding into pleasure, need into need, until she comes—or I come, can't separate our bodies, our release. She arches up, and I thrust deep, and the world dissolves into black sparks.

Whoa. Holy hells! Holy fuck, never felt anything like it in my life.

A phrase that keeps looping in my mind of late.

I understand now Kiaran's dazed grin.

Ariadne breathes something I don't hear, my ears buzzing, my heart pounding. She shifts and I hiss, my cock still lodged deep inside her, every movement sending aftershocks of pleasure through my body.

Carefully, I roll to the side, and she rolls with me until she's curled against me, one leg over mine. My cock gives another appreciative throb.

I could die like this, I think, *and wouldn't mind.*

Then Kiaran molds himself to my back and his scent mingles with hers, sending another pleasurable jolt to my cock.

But before I can do anything about it, Ariadne becomes a dead weight in my arms, claimed by sleep, and Kiaran starts to snore in my ear.

A silly smile spreads on my face. That's worth any discomfort, being surrounded and held by my mates.

I close my eyes and let myself drift.

———

In my dreams, I'm walking on a flat, scorched plain, the earth black and smoking, my feet burning. I have wings on my back, and the shadow I cast is that of a half-beast—pointy ears, claws, and those wings spreading from my back, so large they seem to touch the white sky.

They drag on the ground, leaving grooves behind me. Don't ask how I know, how I see it.

This isn't real, and yet it is. A dream and yet reality, and I know deep in my bones that this means something important, but I can't quite touch it.

What does it mean when more people approach from every direction—men, alphas—all winged? All of them like me, beastly and terrifying, their shadows rushing to meet me before their owners. Our shadows meet in the center, mingle on the ground, churning together.

And then she's there, a pale flame, her wings white, her body entrancing, pale scales covering it, not quite hiding her curves, her breasts, her hips, the dip of her waist, the cloud of her hair, her dainty feet, all that makes her so pretty and desirable, all that makes her mine.

Her affection shines through her eyes as does her need, and I'm dumbstruck, gazing at her, my body reacting to her like every time, in dream and reality, always wanting her.

Then she reaches out to me and her touch shakes me to the marrow of my bones, remaking me, changing me—

"Fuck!" I sit up and almost head-butt Ariadne who's on her knees, reaching for me. Her eyes widen. "Dammit."

"Taj." Her eyes are round in the small oval of her face. "You were mumbling and tossing in your sleep."

"Dreams," I say shortly, then catch her hand before she withdraws it and kiss her palm. "And you? How do you feel today?"

A blush spreads over her cheeks. "Better, thank you."

"We didn't hurt you? You don't hurt down in your—"

"I'm good." Her mouth twitches, and I find myself smiling.

"And Kiaran?" He's gone from my side. I glance around. "Where is Kiaran gone?"

"Over there." She points and I surge to my feet, dragging her along with me, noticing to my sorrow that she's already put her dress back on. "He was there when I woke up."

We find our Wildman standing some way down the trail, at the entrance to the small grove. Tall, muscular, pale, still as if carved from stone.

Buck naked.

Yep, he hasn't bothered with clothes yet and a grin twitches at my mouth as we approach him

"Morning, mate. What's up?"

"Keeping watch," he says. "For Wolves. And Jaguars."

"Of course." I can't fucking believe I slept without taking

any precautions. This desire is dangerous. Makes you lose your mind. I have to organize us better. after all, I am the military man among them. It's my responsibility.

Feeling guilty, I pull Ariadne beside him and she slides an arm around his waist. "Sleep well?"

He glances down at her, then at her hand where it curls over his hip. His cock is stirring, hardening. "Yeah," he says, sounding distracted.

"Me too. I slept like the dead."

"Sex is good," he says, and I snort.

"You fuck like an animal, my man."

Color rises to his cheeks. "Animals fuck good."

"Indeed they do."

It's Ariadne's turn to produce a snicker. She butts her head lightly against his arm and he lifts it, putting it around her shoulders. "Don't mind Taj. Like Finnen, he has certain ideas of how things should be. I like the way you do things."

"You mean, the way I fuck you?"

She chokes a little. "Uh, yes. That's what I mean."

I meet Kiaran's blue eyes over her head and I laugh out loud when he winks at me. "I never said fucking like an animal was a bad thing, you know. In the army, that's an actual compliment."

Ariadne sounds like she's choking again. She may lose herself in passion when we're fucking, but it wasn't long ago she was a devout virginal acolyte. I have two people to break out of their blushing moralistic restraints and retrain in sexual freedom.

I swear here and now that I'll teach her to demand what she wants, to tell me exactly how to pleasure her, and the same goes for Finnen.

Finnen, I hope you hear us and hold on because we're coming to get you, take you back with us where you belong.

22

ARIADNE

Astride our horses, sadly with both my alphas dressed again, we ride direction south, following the river from some distance. We're skirting towns and villages, keeping our eyes peeled to catch a glimpse of the brigade that has captured Finnen.

Kiaran's restless stallion seems even more agitated as we put the miles behind us.

"Stupid horse," Kiaran curses as the stallion dances right and left. "Just walk!"

"Maybe he's smelling something," Taj says, frowning. "Maybe Ariadne's mare or some other mare on the plain is going into heat."

My face starts to burn. "Then why doesn't your stallion act the same way?"

"Maybe he's a gelding. I didn't check."

"Or maybe it's something else," I mutter. "Did you notice how well Kiaran's horse behaved at the gates of the town when he went berserk?"

"Took to the fight like a fish to water," Taj mutters.

"Exactly."

"So what, it likes fighting and now it's bored?"

"No, stupid horse, no!" Kiaran pulls on the reins, and his stallion rears back, almost throwing Kiaran off, but Kiaran's thighs must be like steel, locking against the horse's sides, and he remains glued to the saddle. His glare could set the next town on fire.

"Speaking of gates..." Taj points.

I narrow my eyes. "There's a town on the hill. Which one could it be?"

"By my guess, this could be Staton, one of the last stops before Eremis."

"Last stops?"

"See that smudge in the distance?"

I slit my eyes, Kiaran's horse dancing back and forth at the edge of my vision. "Yeah?"

"That's the Summer Capital."

"We're so close! Shit!"

"*Shit* is exactly right," Taj says grimly. "We need to catch up with the Firebrand Brigade quickly."

"But then where are they? We've been after them for days and not a single sighting." I press a hand to my middle, wincing. "Oof..."

"How are you faring?" Taj asks. "Looks like the pain is back."

"I'll be okay."

"Ari... you have to tell us how you feel. If your heat starts—"

"You'll be the first to know."

"Whoa!" Kiaran's stallion takes off toward the town. "Stop! Stop, wait!"

"Oh hells," Taj mutters. "After him!"

With a sigh, I nudge my tired mare into a gallop and we chase after Kiaran and his stupid horse.

By the time the stallion has slowed down and an irate Kiaran has jumped off, holding him by the reins and walking him around to calm him down some more, we're within sight of the city's flags and of the people passing through its gates along with carts and carriages and horses and donkeys.

Among them, I see something else that makes me loosen a long breath.

"Are you seeing that, Taj?"

"Army banners," Taj says, squinting at a group of riders before the town gates. "Holy shit, it could be them!"

"Can you make the banners out?"

"No."

"Would you recognize the Firebrand Brigade's banners? I didn't see them when they took Finnen."

"I know their banners. They are red with a lizard spewing fire stitched in gold on them."

"A lizard? You mean a dragon?"

Taj shrugs. "Looked like a silly lizard to me."

Kiaran laughs, tugging on the stallion's reins. The wild, open-hearted sound makes me grin.

"We need to get closer," Taj says.

Kiaran swings himself back in the saddle—and the next moment, his stallion whinnies and starts galloping toward the town, him cursing and pulling on the reins in vain.

Again.

I sigh in frustration. Then I blink. "Wait... is the stallion smelling *the Brigade*? Is that why he's acting so weird? Is it possible?"

"It's possible," Taj says. "Army horses are trained to return to the army if they go astray. Maybe he's smelling the piles of horseshit produced by the other warhorses."

"A war horse," I whisper. "Why would the D'Alerys keep a warhorse?"

"Because they have ties with the army, like we guessed?

Doesn't matter." Taj clucks his tongue and kicks in his heels, his horse jumping forward. "Let's go!"

We canter after Kiaran, toward the fortified town, and I cross my fingers that we meet up with Finnen there, at last, and get him back.

———

This town is much bigger than the last one we stayed in, with tall towers on its bastions and a citadel at the top of the hill. As we approach, its fortifications rise over us like mountains, the stone wall surrounding the town core casting a long shadow over the ramshackle houses built outside, at the foot of the hill.

A road leads up to the gate, the line of people and carts slowly moving toward it, while another exits. People cast us curious looks, and when Taj canters up to the guard at the gate, Kiaran and I following him, there's only a handful of complaints from the people waiting.

Confidently, Taj approaches the guards and leans down to ask them a question.

They shake their heads, and my heart sinks.

"Dammit," Taj snarls, throwing me a dark look. "It's not the right Brigade."

"Another one?" Kiaran asks.

"Yeah. This is the Starburst Brigade." He nods at the riders who are standing stoically in line. "As evidenced by their banners."

From up close, their banners are black or dark blue with a star in the middle.

Oh no...

"Let's stay in the town tonight," Taj says. "We're almost out of provisions. Might as well take advantage that we're here and tomorrow our horses will be fresh and fast. We'll catch up with the bastards."

Kiaran shrugs.

I nod, my chest tight, but my belly is cramping pretty badly by now. Resting and eating a good dinner sounds heavenly. Will feeding two of my urgent needs help with the pain or make me feel it more acutely?

Only one way to find out.

"Back to the line!" one of the guards shouts at us and rolling my eyes, I turn my horse around and trot over to stand some way behind the Starburst Brigade.

I won't cry.

We'll find Finnen.

That's a promise.

———

This town smells. It smells much worse than any other place I've ever been. I gag as we ride through the gate and the stench of piss, shit and rot wafts over us. Dark rivulets run through the middle of the streets and people throng the squares and alleys, many hanging out of second-story windows and yelling at each other. Laundry hangs on lines between buildings, and horses and donkeys dump steaming piles wherever they stand, which in turn are rolled flat by the wheels of the carts and carriages.

Oh Goddess... I clamp a hand over my mouth and nose as we walk through the town, looking for an inn. I want a room so I can shut this stench off or I'll die of smell poisoning.

"Don't worry," Taj says as if hearing my inner thoughts. "We'll find a place."

But the first inn we encounter is full, as proclaimed by the sign hanging on its very closed gate.

As is the second one.

"What's going on?" I whisper. "Is there a festival or something we're not aware of?"

"It's just a big town," Taj says, "and very popular with

merchants. There's a deep canal on the other side of the hill that links the town with the river, making it a port."

"What if we head that way? Perhaps there are more inns?"

"I wouldn't. All the drunk sailors will be roaming and every bed will be taken for sure."

Crap.

"We'll find a place," Taj says again, stubbornly.

Kiaran snorts and shakes his shaggy head but offers no comment.

The next inn we find is quieter than the previous ones, and though there's no sign on the gate, once we ride into the yard, a man who has to be the innkeeper walks out to meet us, a dark frown on his face.

"We're full," he says. "Go someplace else."

"There is no other place," Taj says.

Kiaran bares his teeth.

I moan softly, partly in frustration and partly in pain. The heat in my veins has returned full-force and I ache so badly in my belly I could cry.

"Please, good sir." Taj puts on his charming smile that turns him into a lovable rake. "The lady is exhausted and in need of nourishment and a bed. We have coin. We don't need a big room—"

"There are no free rooms. You can eat here," he says, "but there's no place to sleep."

"Please," I whisper. *I won't break down,* I tell myself. *I won't.*

"We don't need much." Taj opens his arms, hands palms-up. "We can bed in the stable with the horses. Just to get out of the cold for the night."

"In the stables. That won't be free," he mutters, giving us suspicious looks.

"Of course not. We're ready to pay."

"Good. Then..." He casts us another suspicious look, lingering on Kiaran. "Leave your horses and come inside to eat.

And stay away from the soldiers. This is their favorite inn, and they've already picked up two fights tonight. May the gods give me patience."

"We will," Taj promises, keeping his grin on, even as my heart starts racing.

What if they recognize Taj? What if they know to look out for us?

Too late to back out now, though, and no other place to go. We just have to keep our heads down, eat, sleep and be on our way.

23

ARIADNE

The innkeeper hadn't been lying. The main hall of the inn is full to bursting with people seated at long tables, eating stew from bread trenches and quaffing beer and mead, shouting and laughing and singing songs with bawdy lyrics.

At least I assume the lyrics are bawdy because the men around the singers slap their hands on the table, roaring with laughter and mimicking the sexual act with their fingers.

It's... interesting. My body heats as it remembers what we did last night, though I still feel embarrassed about it.

About wanting it so badly.

About demanding it.

About feeling the need day and night, even if it's an omega thing I can't control. If I wasn't an omega about to go into heat, would I want it so badly?

And would that be a bad thing? Why should it be? These men treat sex like great fun—and why shouldn't it be? Why should we be taught to keep quiet about it and feel embarrassed at the mention of it?

Lifting my chin, I make a vow to accept my desires. Wanting

my men, wanting the pleasure, the touch, the joining of our bodies is a beautiful thing. I should take a page out of Kiaran's book and not let society dictate how I should feel about this or any other topic.

We take our seat at the far wall, the only seats left because they are the farthest from the roaring fireplace and its warmth. I'm almost in Taj's lap, which makes the fire in me flare, but I grit my teeth and try not to rub myself all over him, because we need to remain discreet and invisible.

Somehow.

Though the soldiers are mostly drunk and busy singing their ditties, I seem to be the only woman in the room.

So *not* good.

I keep my head down as the innkeeper brings us our own trenches of stew and some ale and pretend not to see the looks cast my way. Kiaran is growling deep in his throat, a constant roll of distant thunder, and I swear his hackles are up. Taj is growling, too, I realize, the rumble I feel against my back.

They are alphas. My alphas. And I am theirs.

I just hope for no bloodshed as we dig into our dinner.

Things seem to be going well for a while. The stew is hearty and filling, the ale weak and yeasty. The warmth is a bit too much for me, making me uncomfortable. Sweat trickles between my breasts and down my back, making my dress stick to me, but I can stand it.

Just eat and you can go lie down, I tell myself, *away from all these raucous soldiers and the heat, together with your alphas. They will take the pain away and cool down the heat so you can sleep. Just a while longer...*

"Hey, you!" one of the soldiers calls out. "The wench by the window! Come here, my pretty, come to daddy." He slaps his lap and grins. "Guys, we have a girl to serve us tonight."

Shit.

Soldiers start getting up and turning their heads to see me, yelling at me to join them. A couple actually move toward us, and fear grips me.

Growling, Taj gets up, his arms tight around me. He seats me down and starts toward the soldiers, but Kiaran beats him to it. He's already leaping at them, more panther than man, snarling all the while.

"What the hell?" one of them yelps when Kiaran punches his way through them. "Who is this guy?"

"Berserker!" someone else yells, and chaos erupts.

"Drakoryas!" Soldiers are falling over one another, trying to get out of Kiaran's way, and it's sort of funny.

Even Taj chuckles, though he's standing in front of me like a one-man regiment, ready to tackle any soldier who as much as thinks to come our way. There's a small cushion on the bench and I clutch it to my lap as I watch the show unfold.

Kiaran moves through the room like a whirlwind. Chairs and benches are overturned, trenches go flying, spilling stew everywhere, men fly like puppets through the air and crash, groaning, on the floor.

He grabs two soldiers by their necks. "You don't talk to her," he growls, "you don't look at her, you never touch her. Ever. Understand?" He shakes them. "I said, understand?"

The soldiers nod frantically.

He's panting, blood spattered on his arms and face, pale hair sticking to his neck. "Good. Now stay the fuck away from her."

The innkeeper is staring at us from across the room, eyes round in his white face, a tray loaded with trenchers and ale in his hands. I see him open his mouth, looking at Kiaran, but he seems to rethink it. He just carries the tray to one of the tables, plonks it down, then retreats to the kitchen.

Kiaran releases the two soldiers and wipes his mouth with the back of his hand, then stalks back to us and sits back down in his seat, reaching for his trencher.

As if nothing happened.

"You are a force of nature, aren't you, buddy?" Taj shakes his head with a grin and slaps Kiaran's shoulder. "It's good to have you on our side."

Kiaran's mouth tilts briefly to the side in a smirk, then he goes back to slurping his stew and ale. He doesn't even bother with the spoon the innkeeper provided, lifting the trencher to his lips instead, dripping stew all over.

Finnen would have been incensed at this lack of manners. He'd have snarked at Kiaran, then instructed him how to behave as not to embarrass him anymore.

"What is it?" Taj's gaze is piercing. "Something's bothering you."

"Finnen is also a force of nature," I whisper, suddenly overwhelmed by grief. "I miss him."

"We'll get him back," Taj says, his voice gentling. "Now scoot over. Let's finish eating and retire to our luxurious apartment."

———

"What's that?" Taj asks a while later, after we have indeed retired to our luxurious apartment—in the stable of the inn. Nobody had dared bother us after Kiaran's show of power, and even the innkeeper brought us a plate of stale fried honeycakes afterward, without a word, a frightened look in his eyes.

I bet he can't wait to see our backs. He didn't even ask to be paid in advance.

Yeah, he has to be very frightened.

"Ari..." Taj lifts the lantern he has carried from the dining hall. "What the hell is that?"

I glance down at the small item in my arms. "What? Oh, this? A small cushion."

"Where did you get it?"

"In the dining hall."

Kiaran snorts, walking ahead and scouting the stables for a suitable place to bed down for the night. "Cushion," he mutters.

Taj stops and blinks at me. "Did you steal a cushion from the inn?"

"I didn't steal it," I protest. "I... found it. Someone must have left it there."

"The innkeeper, you mean."

"No, look. It's a lady's cushion." I show him the embroidered flowers and birds on it. "It might be good to rest my head on."

"I want your head on my chest tonight," Taj growls and cups my face, stepping close, so close his body is pressed to mine. "Not on some stupid little cushion."

"Don't insult my cushion," I growl back and he blinks again. His mouth twitches.

"Did you just protect the cushion's honor?"

"*My* cushion," I mutter.

"Hm. And I assume you're taking it with you?"

"Yes, why not?"

"Hm..."

I clutch my cushion to me. Cute little cushion. "What does 'hm...' mean?"

"Nothing." He brushes his mouth over mine, a twinkling in his eyes I can't read. He lifts the lantern again. "Kiaran! Find a good place?"

"Here," Kiaran says from somewhere in the darkness of the stable, and Taj pulls me that way.

"It had better have a good mattress without bedbugs and thick blankets," he says, placing the lantern on the ground.

Kiaran snickers.

I have no doubt I will be warm enough with my men, but we do have the blankets we brought from the D'Alerys house and Kiaran is already spreading one on the hay, close to where our horses are tied, I realize, and shakes out the other two.

I take one from him and pull him down beside me. I wind my arms around his neck, letting the blanket fall to the side.

"My Wildman," I whisper. "What you did was hot."

"Hot?"

"Sexy," I admit. "Fighting those other men off was sexy."

Kiaran's eyes are wide.

"I could have fought them off, too," Taj grumbles. "Don't I get any love?"

I laugh and reach for his hand, tugging. He comes willingly down on the blanket with us, his arms coming around me. "Of course."

Kiaran is frowning. "I always fight for you. No other men touch you."

"Except for me," Taj says. "And Finnen. And..."

"And?"

"We don't know yet if our omega needs more alphas," Taj says quietly, nuzzling my hair.

"How will we know?"

"If she goes into full heat."

I swallow hard. "Let's not think about that tonight. We can't do anything about it now, and I'm tired."

"Are you all right?" Suddenly Kiaran has me lying down on my back, looming over me, and Taj is stroking my hair.

"Feeling okay?" Taj asks.

"I..." I stare up at their handsome faces, the shadows dancing on them in the flickering light of the lantern, and don't know what to say at the concern I find there. My heart flutters in my chest. My belly aches, and having their scent around me makes me ache worse, but at the same time... "I'm okay. I will be, if you lie with me."

"Ari..."

"I need you," I whisper.

"I know," Taj says, smiling. "We're here. We'll give you what you need, right, Kiaran?"

"Anything," he says, and my heart is full.

How did I get this lucky in my unluck?

———

We don't undress fully this time. It's cold, despite the breaths of the horses around us, and I realize it's not necessary when Taj lifts my skirts and simply pulls my undergarments down, to pool around my ankles.

"Are you watching, Kia?" He uses his fingers to spread me wide, and I shiver when the cool air hits the burning, sensitive parts of me.

"A lesson?" Kiaran grumbles. "Now?"

"I'll teach you how to use your mouth on her."

"I *have* used my mouth on her," Kiaran says.

I whimper. The memory of that makes me wetter, hotter. "Yes..."

"That's... interesting." Taj's brows climb up.

"You were saying?" Kiaran is kneeling beside me, his hand inside his pants, working his cock, his breathing uneven, his teeth gritting. "I need to fuck her."

"Remember what I told Finnen about her nub?"

"To circle it." Bitten off. Kiaran's hand is moving faster inside his pants. "Rub it."

"You were listening. And here I thought you were so focused on your cock you couldn't hold a thought in your head."

"Fuck, Taj, if you will only talk, I'll take over."

I open my mouth to ask, *please*, that Kiaran takes over because I can't stand this torture anymore, but Taj leans down and blows warm breath over my spread pussy.

"Oh Goddess..." I moan and try to lift my hips. "Please..."

"Watch," Taj says, and swirls the tip of his tongue around my nub. "This is her clit and it gives her a lot of pleasure." He then drags the flat of his tongue over it, and I arch up with a moan. "Always try to touch it, rub it, when you make love to her. When you fuck her, make sure to press on it, slide over it. Or use your hand to play with it."

"Taj," I breathe. "Please..."

"Enough," Kiaran growls. "Finish it."

24

TAJ

"*Finish it.*"

A shudder goes through me at that harsh command, my cock jerking, swelling more in my pants.

He doesn't know what his tone does to me. Finnen would have done it on purpose. Kiaran is just out of patience.

I lift my head to look at him, his face feral, desire raw in his eyes. He's breathing hard, blue eyes bright with arousal, his body tense with it.

Then I turn my gaze on Ariadne's face and I almost come in my pants from the darkness in her eyes, the flush on her cheeks and chest.

"Fine," I choke out. "Why don't you tell me what to do then, Kia?"

"You want me to tell you?"

"Yeah. Command me. Direct me. Come on."

He doesn't hesitate. "Put your tongue inside her," he orders me, "now!"

Oh fuck.

Another shudder runs through me as I obey, without

thought, my body an instrument of his desire. I use my fingers to spread the rosy lips of her pussy and then I drag my tongue along her seam, lapping at her sweet cream, ending at her cute clit and tormenting it until she cries out my name.

"Make her come," Kiaran commands, his voice hoarse. "Do it now."

How the tables have turned on me, and fuck if I mind. My cock convulses, and I groan. I lift my head to smirk at him, breathless, then I press my lips to her pussy and shove my tongue into her, thrusting as deep as it can go, again and again—

"Taj!" She arches up, coming on my tongue and lips, sweeter than any honey, her hands fisting in the rough blanket —and I shoot my load in my pants, gasping and grunting, acting as much as an animal as Kiaran often does.

Fuck...

"You finished," Kiaran snaps.

"Apologies I couldn't wait for your say-so to come." I shake my head, grinning. "*Sir.*"

"My turn." I raise my gaze to find Kiaran unlacing and shoving down his pants. He pulls out his flushed cock, and it looks painfully hard, veins threading it, the head purple and wet. It juts up, trembling against his stomach, and he grabs it with a grunt. "My way now. I fuck her."

"Just... wait," she pants, then gasps when I take another long lick at her. She hisses. "Wait."

"Too sensitive," I guess, and she nods.

"Yeah." Her cheeks are flushed, eyes fathomless. "A little."

Kiaran frowns. "Done? No sex? You break our omega?"

Ariadne laughs breathlessly. "I just need... some time."

Kiaran groans, giving his cock one slow tug. He grimaces. "Time."

"It's normal," I say.

"Break," he mutters again, scowling at me. "Shouldn't trust."

He often gets like that when he is fighting or aroused, I realize, retreating to his monosyllables and his growling. It's as if normal speech requires too much energy and currently he doesn't have any to spare.

I feel that. It's sticky inside my pants, my cum cooling, and I'm too tired to clean myself up even though I know I have to.

"I think our little omega will get much pleasure from going down on you," I mutter, "won't you, sweets?"

"Go down?" Kiaran looks around the stables. "Go down where?"

"Down on you." I wink at her. "Don't you want to take his cock in your mouth? Tell me you didn't imagine it, wondered about it."

The flush on her cheeks deepens. "I want it," she says. "I can't deny it and I won't. I decided not to be ashamed of my desire, right?"

"That's my girl."

Kiaran groans, his cock jerking in his hand. "In her mouth?"

"Damn right, my man. Imagine how that will feel."

And fuck, why did I have to come in my pants and not experience it myself, first? It doesn't matter. We're a clan, we're a family, and there will be more opportunities, and not to forget, watching is pretty damn exciting, too, especially when you lust after both the girl and the boy in front of you...

25

KIARAN

I'm still trying to wrap my head around the concept of her putting her mouth on my cock when Taj pulls her to her knees and she glances up at me with those pretty, big eyes.

Holy fuck.

I'd never been with a girl before her—hells, I'd never been around people before her, not since I was left in the wilderness, but I think we already did a lot of sex stuff in the time since I met her, and yet...

And yet nothing prepares me for her sweet mouth on my dick. She bends over, her hair sliding over my thighs, her hands gripping my hips, her breath washing over my cock, and then her soft lips brush over the head of my hard-on, making me jerk and groan.

Taj lifts her hair, to watch as she swirls her tongue around my cockhead, a little rough, pointy, hot.

"Good girl," he praises her and she moans, the vibration sending a jolt of pleasure through me, pulling my balls tight. "Now take him in, suck on his cock. Make him come."

Her warm mouth engulfs the head of my cock and slides

lower, and fuck, I almost fall back on my ass at the heat tightening, tightening, swallowing me. Blindly, I grab a fistful of her soft hair, and that makes her moan again, which in turn makes me groan, my balls drawing even tighter, ready to explode.

I need her to take more of my cock in her mouth and I tug on her hair. She chokes, and I'm torn between doing it again and checking if she's okay. There's a haze over my mind, my body taut like a bowstring, hunched over her, as she sucks and licks.

"That's it," Taj mutters, "pull on her hair, use her, Kia. Take your pleasure with her, she likes it. Nicely done... Fuck, that's nice..."

"Dammit." I grunt. If he likes commands, it looks like I like praise.

Like a good dog, I think and scowl, but it feels too good to get really annoyed over it, and besides, seeing how aroused he is from what Ariadne and I are doing is a reward in itself. He's stroking his hardening cock, and I have fucking forgotten how to breathe, looking between him stroking his dick and Ariadne's head between my legs.

Her hands spasm on my hipbones and she swallows around my cock, and my attention is fully on her now, my stomach tightening, my ass clenching. I gasp out her name as I spill in her mouth, rocking, taking my pleasure with her, as Taj instructed.

Feels like a river rushing through me, a fucking river, spilling out of my cock. I swear I feel like the top of my head just exploded.

Black eats at my vision.

I find myself bowed over her, wheezing, Taj's hand on my arm keeping me from falling and crushing her, and one question buzzes in my overtaxed mind.

"Ari, did you...?" I struggle to breathe. "Did you like it?"

She whimpers as I straighten, face red, eyes glittering, lips glistening, and reaches one hand under her skirt, between her legs.

I catch her hand and growl. "No. Mine. "

"But..." She glances from me to Taj and back, a pleading look in her eyes. "I need..."

"I know what you need." I push her back on her ass on the blanket and lift her skirt. "I lick you, you come."

She lets out a strangled sound that's almost a laugh. "Okay, I—"

I spread her legs and then the lips of her pussy, as Taj showed me, then press my tongue right in her center, where she's wet and sweet.

"Kia!" She writhes on the blanket, and I press my tongue deeper, planning on tormenting her small nub right after, but it only takes one lick and press of my tongue for her to come with a cry, her body shaking, her sugar spilling in my mouth.

But it's on my tongue she comes this time, not Taj's, and I grin.

My girl.

My omega.

I found her, and she accepted me, wanted me, kept me. Freed me from my miserable freedom, made me a part of this family.

She may belong to all of us, but she is also mine.

———

Dazed, I lie under the extra blankets, curled against Ariadne's back, her head resting on Taj's chest. He's staring up at the ceiling, or he's asleep already, hard to tell now that we've blown out the lamp, his face a collection of lines and planes, his hair meshing with the darkness.

She is a country of curves and smooth skin. I map her lines, smoothing my hand from her shoulder down her arm to her hand, then over her hip to her thigh. She sighs contentedly and wiggles a little. My hand retraces its route, returning to her hip, then slips over her waist—

And bumps against something soft but coarser than her silky skin.

I lift my head, frowning in the dark. "What's this?"

She turns her head a little. "A cushion," she whispers. "Don't start griping about it like Taj did."

I blink at her. "A cushion."

"A little cushion. Tiny, really. Don't worry about it."

"But why do you have a cushion?"

"I took it from the dining hall."

I wait, but she gives no explanation for her strange action. "Why?" I finally ask.

She shrugs. "I wanted it."

"Okay." I have taken many things I wanted in my life—mostly from trees and animals. I've raided squirrel nests for nuts in winter, *winser* ground nests for sweet maggots, and bird nests for eggs. I stripped trees of all their fruit, chased away wolves from their kill to cut out the best meat. I understand wanting and taking, even if it's not fair.

Stealing, Kia. Robbing. Call it by its name, now that the words are coming back to you.

Fine.

Still... "Is it because you're cold? Are you cold?"

"No, I'm warm and toasty," she whispers, turning her head to smile at me.

So it's not that. Puzzled, I curl more tightly around her. Maybe she *is* cold and won't tell me. I mostly avoid complaining, too, in case they...

In case they leave me.

Dammit.

But she sighs and relaxes against me, snuggling back and

letting out a quiet breath, clutching the little cushion to her middle.

Maybe it hurts, still. Maybe the cushion-thing helps. I barely understand people, let alone girls, and even less a pretty omega who against all odds has proven to be my fated mate.

I understand none of it, but I sure like it. What man in his right mind wouldn't? You don't have to be starved for touch and affection like me to appreciate it, and if you don't... then what can I say? There are always some fucking idiots in this world who don't appreciate anything.

Like I didn't... didn't appreciate what I had so long ago, when...

My lids are damn heavy, my thoughts spiraling, washed away by a river, a river washing through me...

"Appreciate... Appreciate the teachings, Kiaran."

I'm dreaming, floating through bright halls, green trees rustling outside, birds chirping.

"What did philosopher Adrie say?"

"Many things."

"Don't be a brat. Don't be disrespectful. Recite stanza twelve."

"'What I do is a reflection of who I am at any given time. How I react to violence is a mirror of my heart.'"

"'What I give...'"

"'What I give is reflected in others and returns to me.'"

"Returns to me..." The halls dissolve into white mist and the birds fly away as I walk outside and into a garden with a fountain in its middle and a statue of a king holding up a sword, pointing to the sky.

"Home..."

26

ARIADNE

I wake up in degrees to the electrifying sensation of a mouth sucking on my neck, very close to the scent gland. It sends streaks of pleasure down my spine, through my body until it pools in my belly, making me clench.

Oh...

Taj. His scent is unmistakable, smokey and hot, and when he bites lightly, I shudder.

"I want to mark you," he growls against my skin. "Mark you as mine. And be marked by you."

I moan, helplessly. It's the first time any of my fated mates speaks of commitment and it's sexy. It also makes my eyes sting with tears born of relief and happiness.

"I know we have to wait until the clan is complete." He kisses a trail from my neck to my shoulder. "To be sure you have all the alphas you need, but damn... I can't wait to get you pregnant."

I turn my head to stare at him. He's never said anything like this before. None of them have.

Then again, it's still so recent, this thing among us, and it's not long ago they were still struggling with the idea, fighting it, unsure about abandoning their lives up until now and joining me in this mad dash across the land.

I press a hand to my belly, where the now constant ache is waking up with me, tightening my core, and say nothing.

Last night was good, fascinating, eye-opening—but I need them inside of me. Coming on their tongues was amazing, but my body is only interested in one thing right now—and that's getting fucked by their cocks, and his words are fanning the fire.

I want it, I realize, more and more. I want to have their babies. I want to have a house with my nest and grow our family there. It's a primal, raw instinct awakening in me the more time I spend with them, the longer the fire burns in me. I've heard of women's baby fever, but it looks like an omegas' baby fever is worse, an actual fever running through my veins.

I'd forget all about the army after us, Artume and the Temple, the world and its injustices, the Fae and their lost race if I could have Finnen back with us and a place to hide and pleasure each other until we have babies.

Though my mind shies away from the act of baby-bearing. I don't want to think what happens before or after the babies, and that's cowardly, but there you have it. I wish I could snap my fingers and have our babies here with us, cute and chubby and looking like innocent, trauma-free versions of their daddies.

I wish I knew what will happen once they grow up and make their way into the world, or how the world will treat them once it becomes clear that they are Fae-blood, like us. If they will be pursued and imprisoned, tortured and killed.

I gasp, my chest suddenly too tight.

"Where did you go?" Taj traces my face with a finger. "What's on your mind?"

"Nothing. Nothing, I... Kiaran," I breathe, realizing he isn't there. "Where is Kiaran?"

"Dammit. He keeps running off," Taj mutters. "I hope he's not beating up the soldiers from last night."

I snicker even as, to my regret, Taj rolls away from me and sits up, running a hand through his tousled, dark hair, calluses catching on the shiny strands.

"Kiaran!" he calls out, getting to his feet, and I take a moment to ogle his tight backside and broad back. These men are sculpted like works of art. I want to pull him back down, pull out his cock and taste it like I did with Kiaran's last night, stretch my mouth around his girth, explore his hard length, the soft head, lap at the small slit, his taste an echo of his scent, firing me up.

Wrench those tortured sounds out of him as he gets more and more aroused, his cock swelling longer and thicker with every suck of my lips, feel him shake, feel him lose control.

Whew. Shit.

Now I'm wet and he's walking away, looking for Kiaran instead of rolling over me and taking me like I need him to right now.

With a sigh, I sit up and arrange my skirts. My undergarments catch my eye, thrown on the hay a few feet away, stained with my slick.

My nose wrinkles. We need to do laundry. Or buy some fresh undergarments, at least. I hope Taj still has a coin or two left in his pouch.

"I want to mark you and be marked by you."

"I can't wait to get you pregnant."

My heart lurches in my chest and a smile tugs at my lips. Despite my worries, happiness is spreading through me. Maybe today we'll find Finnen and then we can stop running. Yeah, a hiding place sounds better and better. A cave, like the one Kiaran lived in, all fixed up and cozy, or a small house in a hamlet where nobody will know us, where probably nobody even knows the Emperor's name and decrees.

I find my bottines flung some distance away, one of the horses sniffing at them. I dress as best I can, pull hay out of my hair, and go out of the stables to investigate and hopefully locate my men and breakfast.

Who knew sex made you so hungry?

Or maybe it was all the traveling, or this pre-heat tormenting me, but my stomach rumbles loudly and painfully as I exit into the yard of the inn.

———

Dawn has barely broken, and it's drizzling, the clouds dark overhead. Two riders who have just entered from the street are talking with the innkeeper, still astride their horses.

No sign of my men.

Or breakfast.

I open my mouth to ask the innkeeper about either, but he's glaring at me, so I nod at hurry away, in the direction of the dining hall. If there's one thing I've always known about men it's that they can always eat, in fact, they need to eat all the time or they probably die—and alphas are like men on a bigger, more exaggerated scale.

Makes sense that Kiaran would wake up and go in search of food.

But then where is Taj?

The dining hall is warm, the fire burning merrily in the hearth, and the long tables are already crowded. There are loaves of bread in the middle of the tables and each person has a bowl with what smells like the stew from last night.

My stomach cramps with hunger.

Stew sounds good.

Finding my men sounds even better, but where are they? Meeting curious, suspicious stares, well aware that my hair is a nest and my dress all wrinkled and smelly, that my undergarments probably smell like my slick, I make my way deeper into the hall.

And find Taj trying to pull Kiaran off a burly, bearded man who is so red in the face he might be having an apoplexy.

"Ignore him," Taj is saying. "We're leaving today. Let's not have another fight."

"He called me a pointy-eared bastard!" Kiaran says.

"That you are!" the man roars and Kiaran goes after him again. "Fae-blooded freak!"

"We should go," Taj says. "Dammit, Kia. Let go of him, now!"

Growling, Kiaran releases the bearded man who sits back down, smirking. "Freak yourself!"

Disaster averted, Taj drags Kiaran to a table and plonks him down. "Stay here. I'll find some food." He glances at me and his dark brows wing up. "Ari?"

"Yes. Just a moment."

Something has drawn my eye from across the room.

On the back of a bench hangs a soft, light blue mantle with fur trimming, made from wool but finely woven—and in my mind I can see it spread over a bed, or rolled like a candy pillow, the fur warm and slightly ticklish.

I want it.

Need it.

After looking for my men, what I should be doing is put my arms around them, touch them, smell them—but instead I'm mesmerized by this blue mantle, blue like a robin's egg, like a summer sky, looking soft like a baby's skin...

Before I realize, I'm making a beeline for it. Nobody seems to be guarding it, so I lift it off the bench and bring it to my face.

Oh, so soft... I rub my cheek over it. It smells all wrong, but that can be easily fixed. I'll wash it and then let my men rub themselves all over it, saturating it with their alpha perfume.

It will be perfect... for something I can't quite describe. Our bed? Our home?

I turn to go, the mantle in my arms, only to be stopped by a nearly inhuman screech.

"Thief! That's mine, give it back. Thief!"

Oh no...

I turn around to find an older woman in an extravagant blue gown scowling at me, reaching claw-like hands for the mantle I'm holding.

"Give it back!"

"I'm sorry, I..." I look down at the soft mantle. "I need this."

"What are you saying? It's mine." She reaches for it and I take two steps back. "Give me back my mantle!"

"I can't."

"Ari! What are you doing?" Reaching me, Taj grabs my arm and turns me to face him. "What's that?"

"A mantle."

"Give that back."

"No!"

"Gods help me. Why not?"

"I need it."

"What *for?*"

"I don't... know, but it's so soft..." I sigh, somewhere in my mind feeling how ridiculous this is but still unable to let go of the velvety fabric.

"Time to leave," Taj grunts. "Kiaran, come here! We're leaving."

"My mantle!" the woman screeches again, trying to get past Taj to take it from me.

"She doesn't really need it," I reason with Taj as he hauls me bodily away. "She has money. That gown she's wearing is expensive. She can buy another mantle."

"Gods dammit. Think that's an excuse for stealing?" He hustles me out of the hall, grabbing some bread from a table on the way. "Here. Eat this while I saddle the horses. Kiaran, where are you? Ah."

Turning my head, I see him growling something to the screeching woman. She backs away from him, her face going white.

Sudden guilt grips me. Maybe I should give it back. I mean, I know it's wrong to take things from people. "Taj—"

"Too late now," he mutters, hauling me to the stables. "Might as well keep it."

"I don't know why I'm doing it," I choke out. "Goddess…"

"Don't you? All this mess to steal a mantle. I didn't know you had thieving tendencies."

"Let me go," I say indignantly. "I don't have thieving tendencies."

"No? Then what would you call that?"

"I *needed* it," I try again to explain. "It's soft…"

"What would you need it for? We're on the road and you're stealing cushions and mantles. Why are you gathering stuff like a magpie?"

I frown. "I don't know… it felt like something I should do."

It's irrational. I can't explain why. I just know I require it.

"Eat your breakfast." He leaves me inside the door and heads toward our horses. "You're becoming a menace."

My eyes sting. "Please, Taj… I don't understand it myself. I want it for our bed. It needs to be soft and warm and dark and… and…"

He steps out from the stall and stares at me, eyes wide. "Ari… Are you making a nest?"

"Of course not," I scoff, because that would be too much.

"You're an omega," he says. "Omegas like nests."

"I'm not a bird."

"Not, but you are Fae-blood. And the ancestors of the Fae were dragons."

"And they produced eggs," I mutter, annoyed. "I'm not a reptile, either."

He walks up to me, puts his hands on my hot face and I lean into his touch. "No, you're not. But we have been amiss in our duties, us, alphas. Your alphas. Of course you need a nest, and since we haven't provided one for you, you've started gathering the materials yourself."

I swallow hard. "I'm not crazy, then?"

"No more than the necessary amount." He grins down at me, and my mouth twitches. He smooths his thumbs over my cheeks. "The interesting amount."

I let out a breathless laugh. "Is that so?"

"Ah-huh. Now, since we are racing to catch up to Finnen, I can't promise you a nest. But once we get him back, sweets, and we can settle somewhere, I promise to buy you all the cushions and soft fabrics you need for your nest. Do you trust me?"

I nod.

"Good. Now, where the hell is Kiaran? Gods give me strength with that man. Let's get the horses out and throw him on the saddle, tie him there if necessary. If he has picked another fight, I'll kick his ass."

27

ARIADNE

The blue mantle gets bundled together with the small cushion, and I watch like a hawk as Taj ties them to the back of my saddle together with my blanket.

I hate that I'm so out of control, so governed by my omega impulses, but Taj... he seemed to find it normal. Even cute.

I have to stop stealing stuff for my nest.

My nest... What a weird thing. After he said it, I recalled hearing about omegas needing nests, but I never paid much attention. Back then, it all seemed so far removed from me, omegas might as well be people living on the moon.

I never imagined I would awaken and manifest as one.

Never imagined any of this.

"Kiaran!" I leave Taj with the horses and go looking for him. "Where are you?"

Then step back, stumbling a little, as he strides out of the inn, catching my arm and pulling me toward the horses.

"Soldiers!" he snarls.

"What? Where?"

"Inside. Regiment."

"Not the Firebrand Bri—"

"No."

"Shit."

We hurry to our horses, Taj watching us with arched brows. Kiaran's stallion is prancing and pulling on the bridle, foam coating his mouth.

"Military is here," I mutter, grabbing the reins of my mare from his hands.

"Ah. Makes sense Kiaran's horse is so excited." He frowns at the stallion. "Calm down, will you?"

The horse whinnies.

Kiaran takes the reins of his horse and turns to level a dark gaze at the inn. "Fuck."

A group of soldiers comes out, wearing the black and red uniform of the Empire.

One of them walks to the front, his hand on the pommel of his sword—evidently the one in charge. "Who goes there?"

"We don't report to you," Kiaran snaps, his stallion rearing, trying to pull free.

"Shush." I reach out, pat Kiaran's arm. "Hello, officers."

"Your friend there," the man says, "has an attitude."

"Forgive him, lieutenant." Taj has put on his nice-guy smile. "He's as irritable as his horse."

"That's not an excuse," the man says. "And you know your way about military ranks, I see."

I tense. My mare snuffles in my hair. "We had an uncle who was in the army, long ago. My brothers and I are heading out, if you don't mind, gentlemen. It's getting late."

"Heading to Eremis?"

"No," I say.

"Yes," Taj says.

Kiaran grunts.

"It depends," I hedge. "Look, we should get going—"

"Which did you say is your House?" The lieutenant ambles over to us, head tilted back, giving us suspicious looks.

"Oh, you wouldn't know it," Taj says easily, "we moved to the Summer Capital recently—"

"D' Adraj," Kiaran says.

Everyone goes still.

I turn a sharp look on Kiaran. "We just—"

"That's an old and venerable house," the lieutenant says. "I didn't know there were young sons to it."

"We're not," I say. "Sons. Children. We are distant cousins, traveling to meet the family."

The lieutenant nods, still suspicious. "That's a fine stallion you got there. It's the sort of horse we purchase for the cavalry." The stallion rears up when the lieutenant pats his neck. "Then again, this one seems too unruly to have been trained by us."

Phew.

Taj gives the reins of his gelding to Kiaran and comes to stand beside me. "Let me help you mount up... *sister.*"

I nod and when he laces his hands together and lifts me onto the saddle. I arrange my skirts and avoid looking at the lieutenant and the silent soldiers behind him.

Kiaran grumbles something and mounts his horse, too, hauling on the reins. "Ready when you are, Taj."

Just then, the innkeeper wanders into the yard and bows to the lieutenant, then turns a wary eye on us. "Leaving, I see."

"We paid you yesterday," Taj says, testily.

"You stole a mantle from a lady—"

"Rumors and lies. Plus, we paid you enough to reimburse her, if you feel the need." Taj returns to his horse and swings himself up on the saddle. "Now if you'll excuse us, gentlemen. We got places to be."

On impulse, I say, "We're looking for the Firebrand Brigade. Have you come across them recently?"

"They passed by here days ago," the innkeeper says, waving a hand vaguely. "They must have reached Eremis by now."

"Oh shit..." I draw an uneven breath. It catches in my chest, a searing pain. "Oh no..."

"Impossible!" Taj says. "They'd need three-four more days!"

"They said they changed horses in every town, and are galloping fast." The innkeeper shrugs. "They were in a hurry. Said they caught a Fae-blood and wanted to get him quickly to the Summer Capital to be judged and hanged."

I grip the pommel of the saddle until my knuckles turn white, the pain in my chest terrible. "Did you see the Fae-blood they had with them?"

"Yeah, a blind man with long white hair. They said he's a pointy-eared bastard." He shakes his head. "I never thought I'd see the day when the Fae would return."

"The Fae are dead," the lieutenant grinds out. "We saw to that. They were eradicated after the Great War."

"And yet, the Emperor sent you out to hunt for them, didn't he?" the innkeeper says. "My lord."

"The blood has weakened," the lieutenant says. "We're only rounding up anyone who has traces of it, to avoid them rising again. It's a curse, being a Fae, a disease. It can resurface after decades, even centuries, according to the sages. We're making sure no Fae babies are born to keep our Empire safe."

The innkeeper bows. "As you say."

I glance at Taj and Kiaran and see the shock in their eyes, though they have schooled their faces to blankness.

Finnen...

Looks like we have to enter the Summer Capital after all—and we have to hurry the hell up.

———

Abandoning caution, we gallop toward Eremis, skirting villages and farms, the river running alongside us, busy with barges and smaller boats. Time is of the essence, now more than ever. I refuse to acknowledge the cold fear taking residence in my gut. Even the cramps in my belly have taken second place to the numbing panic gripping me.

What if we are too late?

What if we can't save him?

We're really close now, the walls and spires of the Summer Capital rising at the horizon, looming behind the villages and the barges, glittering and towering the nearer we get.

We push our exhausted horses throughout the day, not stopping to rest or eat. The morning drizzle turns to rain, and then in the afternoon, it stops, the wind numbing my skin.

The city rises over us, walls of silvery gray stone and turrets topped with golden caps, reflecting the dim light of the overcast skies.

Kiaran points ahead. "Serpent Gate."

Squinting, I make out two towers and what might be the gate to the capital. "How do you know its name?"

He says nothing, his stallion snorting, and canters ahead.

With a curse, Taj nudges his horse forward, and I follow suit. "Kia!"

When we catch up with him again, I see that he's scratching his arm, a dark frown on his face.

"What is it?" I ask.

He glares down at his arm. Rolls up the sleeve of his shirt. Something glitters there.

Scales.

"You said the Fae came from the dragons," I whisper, glancing at Taj, finding his eyes a little wide. "And the Drakoryas... they are dragon-kin. You have scales on your back, and so does Finnen, on his thigh..."

"We are Fae-blood," Taj says, slowing his horse down, his voice hoarse, "and we're manifesting, one after another. You are awakening the alpha in us, sweetheart, and with it, our true nature."

I pull on the reins. My mouth is dry. "What else do you know about the Fae and dragons, Taj? You have to share that information with us."

"I'm afraid on that matter I know very little," he says and turns his gaze on the Summer Capital. "You know who may know more?"

"Finnen," I whisper.

"That's right. He studied all Fae matters to become a priest. We'll question him, once we get his magnificent ass out of there."

28

FINNEN

The imprints of boots on my ribcage burn like fire. I roll on the floor of my cell and bite back a groan of pain.

I'm fucked.

The military didn't have to know who I am. The moment they saw my ears, they patted themselves on the back and rode straight to the Summer Capital to deliver me for execution and brag about capturing a dangerous Fae-blood.

At least I hope the others are safe and hiding, staying as far away from here as possible.

It's the only thing that kept me sane during the days I spent hogtied on a saddle with no food or water. I threw up a few times, and I'm dizzy as hell.

My ribs are fucking killing me.

It's been... days since I was locked up in here. The first two days I found a cup with water beside me, but that was... yesterday? Two days ago.

My head is pounding a sick rhythm.

This is bad.

This might be my end. At least, when they hang me, I may be too out of it to be terrified. Less embarrassing that way. Though why I'm still clinging to my pride, I don't even know...

I close my eyes, and when I open them, I'm back in the Temple, in the fort, talking with Councilor Kaidan, ice in my belly and loathing in my heart. My eyes are open but is this real?

I go through the rituals of Briareus and Nyx, moving through each position flawlessly and yet aware I'm flawed and doomed to fail. I walk the halls and see lights flashing. The statue of the unnamed god is speaking to me but I can't make out the words. I've failed in everything I have undertaken, and I shall be sacrificed for my sins.

Gods...

Feverish dreams, I think in a moment of lucidity. *It's nothing. Don't pay attention. Either you die or you get better, but don't try to make sense of them.*

Yet they continue, dragging me back under, into dark depths. A jaguar jumps on me, tearing my chest open, sinking saber teeth into my heart, and I try to scream but I fucking can't.

I can't fucking move or speak, my heart hammering. I'm so damn cold, and so alone.

Kiaran, I think, *when you were in the wilderness... I know how you felt...*

Did you also think you'd die alone? That nobody would ever reach out to you, nobody would ever accept you as you are and give you a home?

Yeah. At least I've known parental love and sacrifice, and it changes you, doesn't it? Well, mate, I'm glad I've taken your place. Go in peace, Kiaran, Taj and my lovely Ariadne. Create the family I lost, and remember me as I sink into the cold ground.

———

A voice slowly pierces the layers of ash I'm buried under, slicing through the crushing weight on my chest, the sick pounding in my head.

"Hey. I said, hey! Can you hear me?" A male voice. A poke on my leg. "Are you awake?" Then another poke. "Are you even alive?"

I groan softly and I hear steps shuffle backward.

"You *are* alive. I was starting to wonder."

I wait for the blow to land, tensing all over. The days I spent on the saddle were always followed by nights of pain where I was made an example for something.

For other Fae-bloods, I suppose.

But the blow never lands. Instead, a hand brushes over my sweaty brow.

"You're burning up."

I grunt in reply. I've never been very eloquent and right now I don't think I can even manage speech.

"You should eat and drink," the voice says. "Keep up your strength."

I almost laugh at that. *What strength?* I think. *What for?*

But strong hands lift me to a sitting position and a spoon prods at my mouth. "Come on. It's gruel. I'll see if I can find some medicine for you."

"Why?" I grunt, so curious I manage that much.

"We've all been at the bottom at least once in our lives," he says cryptically and moves away, leaving the darkness to close back over me.

———

"Here," someone says, "drink this."

I choke on the bitter liquid pouring into my mouth, try to push the hand brushing over my chin away. I blink at the darkness.

The cup moves away after I shove it again. "Calm down."

"What is this?" I gasp. "Who are you?"

"Medicine. Didn't I say I would bring you some?"

The male voice from before... today or yesterday? Impossible to tell. I cough, the bitterness lingering on my tongue.

"Awful taste, I know." The voice turns rueful. "But it saved my life once, when a cut got infected and nothing else helped. I'll leave the cup here. You should finish it."

The scrape of ceramic on stone is somewhere to my left. I turn my head that way instinctively—an old instinct formed in a time when I could still see.

"What's your name?" When I don't reply, he sighs. "Look, I'm placing the food here. Here. Hey, are you looking at me?"

I blink, shake my head. The darkness remains the same.

Fabric rustles. He's getting up. "You're blind," he breathes.

"Very perceptive of you," I mutter.

"You are an arrogant, sarcastic bastard, after all," he mutters back and his steps move away. "I'll leave you to your delicious dinner, then."

Panic grips me and I don't even know why. "Wait! Don't go."

He stops. Silence stretches. Then he says, "You should drink your medicine."

I pat the ground to my left until my questing fingers locate the mug. I almost upturn it as I grab it. I bring it to my lips and swallow the whole thing down.

I place the empty mug in front of me, a peace offering, and take a breath.

And freeze.

That scent...

I'm not an omega, why should I care how a guy smells, but I already know I enjoy the scents of Taj and Kiaran, who are my mates as much as Ariadne is, and this man...

"Good," he says simply and lifts the mug, another slight

scrape of ceramic on stone. "Now eat." The wooden tray scrapes more lightly against the floor when he places it in front of me.

"What for?" I whisper, still caught in his scent. "They'll execute me."

"That could take a while. It's the Prince's birthday and they are organizing a big feast."

"Are they?"

He smells like iron and rust, and underneath that, there's a tang of sweet frankincense and white pepper. Is it possible that all Fae-blooded people smell good to me?

Is it possible that his smell doesn't matter?

But the scent won't let me be, and I take another breath, letting the aroma settle within me. Unbelievably, the pounding headache eases a little, enough to let me think.

"Who the hell are you?" I whisper, leaning toward him without any conscious thought.

"My name is Rhian. I'm a servant here. The medicine and food is the extent of the help I can offer you." Again that ruefulness. "Now I have to go chop wood and carry water and light up the fireplaces."

"Rhian..."

"And you?" he asks. "What's your name?"

"I'm Finnen."

"There's something about you," Rhian says as he turns to go. He pauses at the door of my cell. "I don't even know why I want to help you."

But *I* know. I've found another of our fated mates, one who might complete the clan and the bond Ariadne needs. I chuckle quietly at the irony.

"And you're crazy," Rhian goes on. "Great. I've been compelled to help a madman who is sentenced to die."

"Isn't it just funny," I agree, wheezing. "Life is weird like that."

Every time you think you have it figured out, the wheel turns and you find you know nothing at all.

OTHER BOOKS FROM MONA BLACK!

Book 1 in the Cursed Fae Kings series (standalone fae romance novels series):

<u>The Merman King's Bride</u>

A cursed King of Faerie

A princess betrothed to a man she doesn't love

A kiss that will change everything

The last thing Princess Selina expects to find in the lake in the woods is a handsome merman. His name is Adar and he saves her, teases her, kisses her, and tells her she could break his curse.

Because, as it turns out, he's a Fae King, cursed to remain in merman form until he finds a princess to kiss him.

But one kiss is not enough and Selina has other problems.

Such getting engaged to a prince she isn't sure she even likes, let alone loves. Marrying him and having his children is not on her list of favorite things.

And now she's falling for the merman.

He's everything she could wish for in a man. Handsome, protective, kind. Except that he is Fae. And has a fishtail.

Still, she can't stop thinking about him. Keeps going back to him. Craves his kisses.

Would gladly have his babies.

Is this a spell, or is it love? Can she break the curse and save Adar? Will there be a happy ending to their story?

All a girl can do is try. After all, true love is worth fighting for and Selina knows she has found it.

This book is standalone novella-length NA romance fantasy novel, featuring mature situations with some dark themes and adult language. It is a retelling of the Frog Prince, with all the emotions, romance, spice and heat.

———

A completed Paranormal Reverse Harem series! Welcome to Pandemonium Academy!

"Of Boys and Beasts"

One's a werewolf with an ax to grind

Two's a vampire with a heart of coal

Three's a demon with a taste for pain

Four's a fae with a past of woe

Five's a girl who will take them down all

In revenge for the pain they've sown

So what if they're gorgeous? They must atone...

My name is Mia Solace. You know, the girl who will take them down all? That's me.

When my cousin is returned to us by Pandemonium Academy in a glass coffin, in an enchanted sleep she isn't expected to wake up from, I grab her diary and head to the academy myself.

Because her diary, you see, tells of four cruel boys who

bullied her and broke her heart until she sought oblivion through a spell.

Four magical boys, because that's the world we live in now, heirs of powerful families attending this elite academy where the privileged scions of the human and magical races are brought together in the noble pursuit of education.

As for me, I cheat to get on the student roster, and once I'm in, well... it's war, baby. I'll get those four sons of guns, steal their secrets, make them hurt. I'll transform into an avenging angel for my cousin, for all the girls they've wronged, and I bet there are plenty of those.

While growing up, my cousin was my only friend. Now I'll be her champion.

Only these boys aren't exactly as I pictured them. Devastatingly handsome, deliciously brooding, strangely haunted, they're getting under my skin and through my defenses.

Kissing them surely wasn't part of my plan...

Getting into bed with them even less.

———

Do you like contemporary RH omegaverse? Check out my new series The Candyverse. Start with book 1: Bee and the Honey Crew (The Candyverse #1)

Bee Robinson's dream is to be an omega. What she is, though, is a weird beta on the run from her ex and her small town.

Weird as in *unusual*, as in being a lot like an omega, rather than her official designation. It's what got her into trouble with her ex and her family.

But now she's about to get her life straightened out. A new town, a new job, new friends, and a chance to accept who and what she is.

Learn from your mistakes, isn't that what they say?

What doesn't kill you makes you stronger.

Only her new friends also seem to think she may be an omega, and so do the members of the St. Laurent pack who instantly start courting her.

A pack of four gorgeous males, each with their own insecurities and doubts, a pack needing her to cement the bonds that make them a family, needing her to join them as their mate.

A family...

Does it matter if you're a beta or an omega when all you need is to accept yourself as you are and see where it takes you?

Her new friends and the pack seem to think so, and in the end Bee may have to let nature take its course, come what may.

At the end of the rainbow, there will be a happy ending.

––––––––

Or maybe you like dystopian paranormal RH omegaverse? I have you covered, too. Try my series Golden Cage Omegas – and start with book I: Caged

Finding out I am an omega in a world ruled by betas was only the beginning of my troubles...

Alphas and omegas are considered non-humans. We're thought of as animals, some of whose traits we share. Furry ears and tails, anyone? Oh, and also mating cycles. Finding out I am an omega in a world ruled by betas was only the beginning of my troubles...

That's right.

Not something I thought I had to worry about. See, I thought I was a beta. I thought I was human.

And then, my world is upended once again when my

parents are killed by a pack of rogues. Escaping, I head to the city, and there I am captured and sent to the Golden Cage.

A Cage where omegas are kept, to be sold to an alpha pack. To the highest bidder.

I came to the city to find a gang of boys I met many years ago, to beg them for help, but instead I am being sold to an unknown pack, the choice not up to me.

———

Do you like dark paranormal romance? Do you like fairytale retellings?
Try my completed Brutal Never Boys trilogy!
King of Nothing (Brutal Never Boys 1)

No man has ever managed to satisfy me—until Peter Pan carries me away to Neverland and now all bets are off...

I never thought that there is another reality beyond this one. My life is normal—work, routine, a few disappointing flings—when a man grabs me from the street and carries me off the Neverland.

A madman.

Granted, he probably saved my life, and the island he has brought me to is beautiful, the sights including three more hunks like him.

He says his name is Peter Pan and this is Neverland, he says they have been waiting for me and I may be the one...

Yeah, he sounds like a madman, all right.

A pity. He's so pretty. And so are his friends.

Peter and the Lost Boys, living on an island where the mermaids sing in the sea and creatures named Reds roam the land.

It sounds like a fairytale.

But if Peter is mad, the rest aren't much better. Dark forces seem to be at work here, and I'm caught in a web of fear and doubt.

The Lost Boys turn out to be violent, vicious men and I am their plaything.

Caught in a web of desire and pleasure.

Am I really the one they have been expecting?

Can I save them?

And do I even want to?

ABOUT MONA BLACK

Mona is a changeling living in the human world. She writes fantasy romance and reverse harem romance, and is an avid reader of fantasy and paranormal books. One day she will get her ducks in a row and get a cat so she can become a real author.

Check out her paranormal reverse harem series Pandemonium Academy Royals, and her fantasy romance series Cursed Fae Kings.